Mars Transit

V.J. Quinn

Exile Creek Publishers

ISBN 978-1-7341138-0-8

Every ship must have a name, and the ship that would bear Sol Vincente to Earth had been dubbed *Speedy*. Sol liked the name.

Sol rendezvoused with the *Speedy* in high Mars orbit, having been lifted there by a small commercial shuttle called the *Santa Cruz*.

Sol hesitated only an instant before entering the living quarters allotted him on the *Speedy*. Cramped though the *Speedy* might be, the coffin-sized passenger cabin of the *Santa Cruz* was surely worse, far worse.

Sol's claustrophobia had already been hogtied and gagged by a well-balanced mix of benzodiazepine-like drugs and alcohol: his otherwise uncontrollable fear of closed spaces could do no more than make ineffectual mewling sounds from the back of his cottony mind.

Jana was already there on board the *Speedy*. She was seated, fully-clothed, on a couch. She showed none of the intriguing self-confidence of her catalog images.

Sol found that he could not focus on her. Instead, his eye was drawn to the couch, which practically circled the room, drastically cutting down the available floor space, hence cutting down the overall sense of space. Above the couch, the promised eight-foot ceiling sloped alarmingly toward the perimeter of the passenger cabin, to a height of just more than four feet, so that your head was bound to nearly bump the ceiling when you sat on the couch.

Also, the room was not a twelve by twelve square, as promised; instead, it was a circle or perhaps an oval — Sol's perceptions were a hopeless blur — probably no more than ten feet across at its narrowest.

Sol struggled weakly to protest as they strapped him into a specially widened and cushioned section of the couch. The space was too small! — He would never survive the trip! — This was not what he had bargained for!

Jana hovered over him. She pecked him on the cheek. "Thanks," she said.

"For what?" Sol asked, blinking rapidly, alarmed and drowsy at the same time.

"For taking me with you." She gave him a tense smile; "For taking me home."

The technicians strapped Jana in beside him, then faded through the exit hatch.

There was a sudden hum which rose to an enormous roar. The lights in the tiny living space flickered and dimmed. The slight artificial gravity, caused by the rotation of the *Speedy*, ceased for an instant, then began to pull from a new direction. The g-force became intense, intolerable. Some monstrously powerful, spectral hand grabbed Sol and attempted to squeeze his brain, his heart, his lungs, most of all his stomach sideways through his skeleton, his skeleton through his skin.

Sol blacked out.

Sol Vincente would never regret his time on Mars. On the other hand, he was happy to sell off his villa and his vineyards, his sand yacht and his servants — all of the comfort items — to pack his bags or, rather, to have his bags packed for him, and to return home to Earth.

Mars was still too much of an unformed frontier.

He planned to keep his extensive land holdings in Hellas Planitia, where all the development action was now, where the vast dome was partially functional and nearing completion, and in the other promising lowlands, Isidas Planitia and Argyre Planitia, where, he believed, whole cities would spring up in the near-future. Hellas, he was sure, would pay off handsomely in his own natural lifetime. The profits to be made at Isidas and Argyre were for his children and grandchildren and for future clones of himself.

Sol Vincente was eighty-one years old. But he had the physique of his father at age forty-five. He had the physique of his grandfather, who had actually been born as far back as the Eisenhower administration, at age thirty-five.

Sol's life expectancy was one hundred twenty-five years. The same as everyone else in his income bracket. With all the drugs and genetic enhancements, you stayed young, relatively young, until you hit one hundred, then actively middle-aged until you hit one hundred twenty, one twenty-two. At which time you hit "the Wall." After that, horrific decline: death, on average, in three to five years. After the Wall, the lucky ones were the ones who did not outlast the average.

Barring further medical advances, Sol had a mere forty years left before his own encounter with the Wall, and so he had determined to live his last productive years on Earth, where the quality of life – the culture, the contacts, the travel opportunities – was still so much richer. To be sure, he would miss a few things about Mars: the wide-open, free-wheeling competition to acquire and develop land, the sense of being on the spot at the beginning of a vast new human adventure, the sense of being a kind of trailblazer, a history maker. Those were the big things Sol knew he would miss about Mars. On a far less exalted plane, Sol had just begun to grow accustomed to and to take full advantage of Mars' peculiar laws regarding the ownership of servants — laws the people back on Earth regarded as primitive, barbaric, atavistic.

He booked a first-class private flight from Mars to Earth: eight days. Eight days! Amazing. Typical flights between Earth and Mars still followed the standard Hohmann minimum energy trajectory: two hundred sixty days, give or take. Eight and a half months!

He opted for all the upgrades. Sol was claustrophobic and so demanded, at any price, the largest living space possible. This turned out to be 12x12x8, by the old standard of measurement Sol still felt most in tune with, as well as a Lilliputian bathroom and shower. Anything larger increased travel time dramatically. (Sol didn't understand the first thing about the science of slip-speed travel, but every leading expert assured him this was so.) Sol shivered to think of spending eight days in such a space, with no possibility of escape.

He paid to have installed a limited capacity HyperWorld™ device. It took up the same space as the bathroom and shower: you flipped a switch, the plumbing fixtures retracted, and the holographic machinery began to whirr. The limited capacity model was a far cry from the deluxe HyperWorld™, in which Sol had spent countless enjoyable hours at his Martian villa. But the deluxe model was simply too big and too heavy for interplanetary slip-speed spaceflight, even for a man of Sol Vincente's resources.

Sol knew from personal experience, trying out the limited capacity model in the manufacturer's showroom, that it was no more than a glorified treadmill. But Sol felt he had to have it.

Of course, Sol stocked his ship's cabin with vast quantities of alcohol and tranquilizing drugs: additional protection against his claustrophobia.

Of course, he hired a female companion.

The woman he hired was named Jana. He did not know her last name. Last names weren't provided in the electronic catalog where he found her.

As far as Sol could tell, every other woman in the catalog was a "professional." Perhaps a few did some legitimate modeling. But by and large these women made their living by hiring themselves out to be used for the pleasure of wealthy individuals. "Space companion" was simply one of many services they offered. Not all of the women in the catalog were strangers to Sol Vincente: he had hired a few of them in the past, for a night or a weekend. They were all, without exception, ravishing.

Jana had a different look about her. She was certainly pretty in a girlish sort of way, beautiful even, and un-self-conscious about it: direct blue eyes, freckles. Her hair was straight and unadorned, a shade too brown to be called blonde, simply cut and tied back in an artless ponytail, so that the ragged end of the ponytail did not quite reach to her shoulders.

What had particularly caught Sol's eye was how natural and un-posed Jana looked in her catalog images. The other women displayed themselves in videos of at least semi-professional quality. These videos generally followed a similar format: the woman started out costumed in something alluring or eye-catching, she did a slow strip-tease while speaking directly into the camera — "I so much want to please you": that sort of thing — then, naked, moving rhythmically, massaging herself in all the places a client would want to fondle, she struck a series of sensual poses, rather like a gymnast or a figure skater going through the required elements portion of a competition. For Sol, watching these videos, one after the other, the effect was at the same time arousing and tiresome.

Then he happened on Jana. Her images were presented not as a video performance but as a slideshow: simple, well-lit photos of her sitting on a couch, unabashedly naked. Sol had never seen a woman who was at the same time so young and so comfortable in her nudity. Even the most experienced of the "professionals" could not appear naked before a camera without some hint of it in their eyes: some gleam, some haughtiness, some challenge. But this Jana simply gazed back at you over the top of those girlishly freckled high cheekbones.

The text of her catalog entry was brief and to the point: "Earth-bound space companion only. Jana offers no other service. This girl really just wants to go home!"

Sol was bothered by the fact that there was no video footage of her. He liked to see how a woman moved before he hired her. For that reason, he did not choose Jana immediately. He kept scrolling through the other catalog entries but, time and again, he found himself staring into the unstudied openness of Jana's blue eyes.

Sol initiated his order for Jana through the electronic catalog. For a small retainer, he was able to place a hold on her schedule for the required dates. But, it turned out, a space companion arrangement was more complicated than Sol's usual woman-for-hire dealings. A full contract for services was required, as per one of the recent Terran/Martian treaties of law.

Sol called his senior attorney and told him to work

out the details.

"And make sure she's legitimate," Sol said.

After a sour pause, Sol's senior attorney asked, "What, exactly, do you mean by legitimate?"

Clearly, the man was not happy to be given this chore, but Sol Vincente was too powerful a client for even this high-status lawyer to outright object.

"Here," Sol said, pecking away at a keyboard as he spoke. "I'm sending you a link to her catalog page. Find out if there's any truth to this business about a girl who just wants to get home. I understand she's not requesting return travel expenses to Mars, which any other of these Martian catalog girls would want as a matter of course. But maybe the whole thing is a come-on, you know? Maybe this Jana plays the game from both ends. Once back on Earth, maybe she becomes the beguiling innocent who would do anything to get to Mars. Maybe she specializes in these Mars-Earth, Earth-Mars flights. I'll probably still hire her, even if that's the case. But I'd just like to know the true picture. Keep me posted. Thanks."

And with the flip of a finger, Sol Vincente terminated the discussion.

Two days later, Sol received an electronic message from his senior attorney:

Attached please find a contract for services. It requires your signature and/or initials in various flagged locations. Please sign and/or initial and return to my office. As requested, I have made certain enquiries. Based on the information available to me at present, I have no reason to doubt the subject's representation.

To which Sol responded: *I'm assuming your last sentence means that this Jana girl is for real. How much extra do I have to pay to get a lawyer to say something in plain English?*

To which Sol received no reply.

Jana smiled down on him. The room was dimly lit. Her face, reflecting the feeble light, was a brilliant pearl in the heavens.

Sol moved to touch her face but found his hand restrained.

"How do I get out of this?" he said, realizing he was still strapped in.

"There's a key pad beside your right hand," she told him. "And there's a video screen on the ceiling just in front of you. Can you see it?" She bobbed her head sideways to be sure she wasn't in his way.

"Yes yes," he said wearily. "I see it."

"Just punch in the code, and the straps will let go."

His hand was shaky. He kept pressing the wrong keys.

Jana put her face next to his, cheek to cheek, so that they were both looking at the screen. She smelled of lemon and lavender and of Martian dust. Sol felt her hand slide down his right arm, over the back of his hand, felt her take control of the key pad.

She made a few quick finger stabs, and Sol was free.

Sol barely had room to pace. One, two, three steps, and then half a step more, before the blasted circular couch bumped his knee. It was intolerable.

The gravity was not right. The ship was supposed to settle into a constant acceleration to keep the g-force at no more than twice as strong as Martian gravity. That would still put it at something like eight-tenths of Earth gravity. Anything less than one-gee, Sol had read, ought to help reduce an Earth-born claustrophobe's misery. But the gravity on board the little ship had to be more than a gee. Had to be, Sol was sure of it.

Of course, the *Speedy* was entirely computer controlled: there was no captain, no crew to question, and no way to interface with the computer. Propulsion, navigation, life support, it was all sealed off from Sol, who wouldn't have had an inkling how to adjust any of these systems in any case. God, was he trapped!

And the ceilings. No way was any part of the ceiling eight feet high, as promised. No way. Standing in the center of the cabin, Sol could reach up and touch the ceiling, and he was not a tall man, not more than medium height.

He pushed on the ceiling with the pads of his fingers. "Is the ceiling getting lower?" Sol asked Jana with some alarm. "I think it's getting lower."

Jana looked up from the notebook screen Sol had given her to read.

"I'm sure it's not."

Sol croaked, "I don't think I could touch it so easily a minute ago."

"Should I get you a pill, Mr. Vincente?" Jana asked.

"Shut up and keep reading," Sol growled.

Finally, there was the trouble with the girl, this Jana.

The trouble started less than an hour after they came out of their initial high-acceleration stage.

Feeling the need for a little distraction, Sol said, "Take off your clothes."

Jana was aghast. "Take off my...?"

"Yeah," Sol said. "I think I'll watch you move around a while then maybe you can give me a nice blowjob or something."

Jana paled.

"Something wrong?" Sol asked.

Incredibly, the girl claimed not to understand what was required of her as a space companion. Sol was sure she must be putting him on.

"It's all spelled out in your service contract," he told her, once he began to see that she might be serious.

She claimed that she had never read the contract, that the agent at the booking service had given her a big stack of forms to sign and told her it was all routine, nothing to worry about.

"He seemed so honest," Jana said.

Sol still couldn't quite believe it. "What about the photos?" he demanded.

Sol had the nude catalog photos of Jana saved to his notepad, along with her contract, and he brought the photos onto the screen. Seeing them, one after another, Jana blushed uncontrollably, seemed on the verge of tears.

"That's me," she said. "I remember when the agent shot those pictures, I remember sitting on that sofa, but I never took my clothes off."

"Are you saying they pasted another girl's body in? I don't believe it. I always run diagnostics on any image out of that catalog before I place an order."

Jana said, "No, I'm not saying it's another girl, it's me all right, it's my body. It's exactly how I look. I have a mole exactly there and another one there." Her finger touched the screen. "Those are my..." ("Breasts," she would have said, but embarrassment overcame her.) "And that's how I look...down there. But I never... It can't be. Please turn it off."

Sol ignored her. He pecked at the keyboard while her photos rotated through a slideshow loop.

"If these have been doctored in any way, it's very impressive, it's a technology I've never seen before. And you say it *is* your body?"

"Yes. Please turn it off."

Sol paused the loop so that a single picture of Jana remained on the screen: the one where she sat with her feet up on the sofa, soles together, knees far apart, her hands not quite covering her crotch.

"You know what I bet?" Sol said. "I bet that nice, honest agent also got you to sign an unconditional medical release form. That would give him complete holographic access to every scan, every examination you've ever had. You really ought to read a thing before you sign it."

Sol clicked a few more keys. The image of Jana disappeared from the screen, replaced by text.

"Here," Sol said. "Here's your service contract. I think you'd better read this now."

When she was done reading, Jana looked up, tears in her eyes.

Sol waited.

"Could you maybe just…" she hesitated, "could you send me back to Mars?"

Sol burst into laughter.

Jana couldn't see what was so funny; she tried to make sense of it. "I don't mean now, I know that's not possible. I mean, after we get back to Earth."

Sol laughed even harder.

Jana persisted, "I think it would be fair. You wouldn't get, um, what you wanted out of the deal but neither would I."

Sol flopped onto the couch and laughed himself out. When he was done, he said, "Sweetie, do you have any idea what it cost me to include you on this flight?"

Jana began to answer, but Sol held up a hand. "I'm not talking about what you're supposed to get paid in the contract. If I paid you ten times that much, a hundred times, it would still be peanuts. I'm talking about the cost to carry your weight at this speed from Mars to Earth. It's astronomical, no pun intended.

"And so you think a good solution here is for me to give up what I'm supposed to be getting out of this deal and to spend even more money sending you back? Obviously, if I did it, you'd go by regular transport: eight and a half months. But still, even at that speed, the cost is huge. Why do you think it's all pretty much one way from Earth to Mars?

"No. There's really only one thing to do. I'm delivering on my side of the deal, you have to deliver on yours."

"You could have them throw me in jail," Jana offered, "for reneging on our contract."

Sol laughed again. "Yeah right, and you could say, 'He's off his rocker – he shtupped me the whole time.'"

"I promise I wouldn't say that. I'd tell the truth. I'd let them put me in jail."

Sol was suddenly thoughtful, almost downcast. "Am I such a horrible old man you'd go to such lengths not to fuck me?"

"No no, not at all, Mr. Vincente. You're... I think you're handsome, and very sure of yourself, but not arrogant or anything, or not too arrogant, not arrogant in a bad way, I mean, you're just very confident in yourself." She seemed to be searching for other words. "You're virile," Sol hoped she would say; "You're any girl's dream." But the best she could finally mumble was, "You're a cool dude." When had young people started saying *that* again?

Sol asked, "So what's the problem?"

With awful difficulty, Jana looked Sol in the eye, pleadingly. "The problem is I'm a virgin and I've made a pact with my boyfriend back on Earth. He's my soulmate. I'm saving myself for him and he's saving himself for me."

At least she was amusing, he had to give her that. He didn't know which was funnier: "He's my soulmate" or "He's saving himself for me."

When he finally stopped laughing again, Sol asked, "So, how old is he, this boychik of yours?"

"Twenty-seven."

"Twenty-seven?"

"Well almost. He'll turn twenty-seven next week. I was hoping to surprise him. He doesn't know I'm coming home. I was hoping that we would give ourselves to each other on his birthday."

Twenty-six, twenty-seven, what did it matter? It was ludicrous, hilarious, but Sol unexpectedly found himself beyond laughter.

"Sweetie," Sol said with the utmost gentleness, "if he's twenty-seven, or soon to be, and he's got a dick attached, he's not a virgin."

Whatever surprises she was planning for her soulmate, Jana surprised Sol now by springing to her feet. She walked two paces away from him, more than half the room, turned and began to unzip her flight suit.

The flight suit fell away from her body to reveal a skin-colored bra and white cotton panties. Jana hesitated, deeply embarrassed, before lowering the straps of her bra and baring her breasts. Her breasts were small but _eautyfully shaped, with tight, brownish, slightly up-turned nipples, and there were the two moles just like in the photos.

Jana wheeled the bra on her upper belly until the clasp was in her hands. She opened the bra and dropped it to the floor. *There really just isn't an elegant way to get a bra off a woman*, Sol mused.

Jana did a much better job with the panties. She tried once, then twice to pull them down while facing him; she couldn't bring herself to do it. It was the sexiest strip-tease Sol had seen in years. Finally, Jana turned around and the panties slowly, slowly slid down to reveal her absolutely perfect ass. The catalog photos had all been of Jana sitting on a sofa and so none had captured this spectacular sight. Jana's ass was the perfect balance between tautness and roundness, between girlhood and womanhood.

Sol's penis stood at attention. The panties were on the floor, curled around Jana's ankles like a lazy, white snake. Jana stepped out of them and turned.

"Don't cover yourself," Sol urged but Jana couldn't help herself: she clutched at her pubic hairs with both hands. Her hunched shoulders, her rigid arms only served to gather up her quivering breasts and put them all the more on display.

Sol sighed. "How old are you?" he wanted to know.

Her clear, frank, blue eyes, which had so captivated him in her catalog photos, now flashed anger, distress, embarrassment.

"You must already know," she all but accused.

"From the catalog? Oh please, I never trust those things, even less so now. I know how old they say you are but I want to hear it directly from you. How old are you?"

"Twenty-one," she said.

"Apparent or real?" But this only confused her. "Were you truly born twenty-one years ago?" Sol clarified.

"Of course," Jana answered.

"Put your hands to your sides," Sol said, and reluctantly she obeyed him. "What a sight you are," he said. He stared at her and she could not bear to return his gaze.

Jana began to speak but so softly Sol had to interrupt her, had to ask her to speak up.

"Is there any way," she repeated, "that I can fulfill my contract with you, Mr. Vincente, sir, which I freely acknowledge I signed and am bound to keep, and also be true to my boyfriend?"

"Your promise to your boyfriend was what, exactly?" Sol asked, the dealmaker in him sensing middle ground.

Jana said, "My promise was that, when he and I made love for the first time, I would be a virgin."

Sol said, "Why don't you get us both a glass of red wine and let's discuss this idea of yours — what it means to be a virgin?"

There were no glasses on board the *Speedy*. Drinks came out of vacuum packed plastic containers, even vintage wine. Sol and Jana sipped Mars' best brunello through tiny plastic straws.

Jana was hard to pin down on the meaning of the word "virgin." Not that she was being evasive, she just didn't seem to have given it a great deal of thought. To Sol this eagerness to promise something she couldn't define was yet another manifestation of Jana's tendency to sign things she hadn't read.

Jana's starting point had been: "It means no sex."

Sol asked her to describe the act in detail but embarrassment or ignorance or some combination of the two prevented her.

"Kiss me," Sol said.

Startled, Jana gave him a tentative peck on the cheek.

"On the lips," Sol demanded.

The fact that she was sitting there nude in front of a fully-clothed man, a somewhat older man at that, made Jana perhaps more submissive than usual. She brushed his lips with hers, holding her hands just below her chin, covering her beasts with her forearms.

"Again," Sol said and, when she leaned forward to kiss him again, Sol cradled her head with both his hands, prolonging the kiss. Slowly, he ground his lips against hers. He slipped his tongue between her lips but she remained tense, blocking the progress of his tongue with her teeth. Finally, he let her go.

She gazed at him fearfully, obviously expecting him to spring on her and to take her by force in the next instant.

"Was that sex?" Sol asked. "Are you still a virgin?"

"Yes," Jana said, then, "I mean no. No it wasn't sex and yes I'm still a virgin."

"Good," Sol said. "Drink some more wine, let's keep experimenting. Do you know what a lapdance is?"

She did not.

Sol directed her. Jana straddled his lap and squirmed. Sol kept his dick in his pants, thinking that sooner or later she'd loosen up a little and start moving more rhythmically, more sensually. It didn't happen. Instead, Sol began to feel closed in, pinned against the back of the couch as he was, with Jana taking up so much of his field of vision and the cramped space of the cabin looming in every direction.

Frantically, he pushed her off.

"Did I hurt you?" she asked solicitously.

"No dammit!" Sol said. Then, between shallow

breaths: "Get me a pill — one of the blue ones — and another glass of wine, hurry."

It took her a moment to understand his difficulty but once it registered Jana sprung into action. Sol caught a glimpse of the uninhibited girl he thought he had hired. Watching her move, thoughtless and naked, was a partial distraction for Sol from his fears.

The drugs and the wine were having their effect on Sol. Panic was pushed to the back of his mind. He had suggested that Jana take a pill, too: "to relax yourself," he had said.

"I don't think the contract says I have to do that," Jana had replied.

Sol was too mellowed out to bother making the point that Jana should be the last person to insist on a strict enforcement of their contract, although he was still clear enough in his mind to think it.

Instead, he urged her to keep enjoying the excellent Martian brunello. She was just starting on her third.

"Dance for me," Sol ordered. She tried but she was no good at it, a little too drunk and at the same time too self-conscious.

"Come here," Sol said. "Sit beside me."

Jana sat.

"Show me your pussy."

She gave him a shy frown, but she obeyed. Her sparse, unshaved pubic hair was tightly curled, a darker shade of brown than the hair on her head.

"Touch yourself," Sol said.

Slowly, as she fingered herself, Jana's frown became an exquisite pout.

"Make yourself come."

This distressed her. "Please, Mr. Vincente, don't make me do that," she pleaded.

"Why not?" Sol was genuinely curious.

"It's not...it's just not something a nice girl does to herself."

"Nonsense," Sol said. "Anyway, you've done it before, haven't you?"

Jana gave no reply. Her fingers glistened with vaginal juice. She blushed uncontrollably.

Sol persisted, "You can't tell me you've never masturbated. You're not telling me that, are you?"

Reluctantly Jana said, "No, sir, I'm not telling you that."

Sol began to point out that, of course, a girl could masturbate and still be a virgin, and, in fact, if she could not, then Jana's promise to her boyfriend was already void, but before Sol could get the first words out, Jana came.

It was so simple and so sweet, the way she came. She made a quick little noise in her throat, sort of like the sound a person might make if she had just remembered a pot of water left boiling on the stove. She narrowed her eyes to slits for an instant, then opened them wide and stared at the ceiling as if enraptured by some deep harmony only she could hear. *The music of the spheres*, Sol thought. Jana shuddered, quietly and with the utmost contentment, something almost akin to the purring of a voiceless cat.

She shuddered again and again and again and again.

After a moment of reverent silence, Sol said, "Do me like that," like a kid begging for the next ride on a carnival pony.

Jana was clearly mortified.

Too bad, Sol thought. He could see her working it

out in her head just as he had already worked it out in his: if she could masturbate herself and be a virgin, she could, by his lights, just as safely masturbate him.

He might have ordered her to take his dick out of his pants, almost did. But his dealmaker instinct held him back: they were still seeking the middle ground of this arrangement; this was not the time to throw his weight around, to make demands that might be interpreted by the other side as demeaning; this was the time to be partners or to pretend to be partners, the time to make a show of working things out together.

Sol stood up, unzipped his standard-issue flight suit, let the paper-thin garment fall to the floor. He wore nothing underneath. Why bother with inessentials when every ounce of payload equaled substantial cash?

Sol was already semi-hard – in his grandfather's time, even in his father's time, this would have been a noteworthy achievement for a man of Sol's real age. In the here and now, it was a common enough occurrence for Sol Vincente. But then in the here and now, a man's real age mattered far less than his apparent age, provided of course that he was wealthy enough to afford the full package of age-defying chemical and genetic treatments – (apparent age enhancement without performance enhancement was available for cheaper).

"Do me like that," Sol said again, a quiet plea this time as he settled onto the couch, his dick pronging.

Jana had masturbated herself with her right hand and that hand rested still on the smooth, pale skin below her navel and above her meager, girlish bush. Slowly, she reached out with her left hand, touching the shaft of Sol's penis ever so gently with the tips of two fingers. Slowly, shyly, her fingers stroked up and down. Sol's gaze moved from those delicate, tentative, lovely fingers along her lightly-freckled bare arm and shoulder to the plain, unaffected beauty of Jana's face. How to describe the expression of her face? It had something of a frown about it, something of a pout. She wore a look of determined, somewhat distressed concentration, as if she were carefully studying his now quite swollen penis. Sol's gaze slowly wandered from her face, lingering to admire her compact breasts, her tight ever-so-slightly upturned nipples, still brownish but now also glowing a rosy pink; from there his gaze returned to her freckled, downy arm, her fingers and thumb now circling his cock, moving up and down in a slow, dream-like rhythm. Her hand was dry but her touch was so light that there was hardly any chaffing.

Sol spoke in little more than a whisper. "It needs some lubrication."

She didn't seem to understand, and Sol placed his hand on hers, lifted it to her lips, and told her to lick. She was appalled, almost repulsed, but his tone of voice left no room for refusal. She licked. He replaced her hand on his dick.

Her hand moved from the base of his penis to just below the corona. She seemed to have some kind of aversion to the tip. From time to time he had to tell her to lubricate. She obeyed, more or less, quietly spitting on her fingers instead of licking.

He turned slightly toward her while she stroked him, so that his own hands were free to stray to her breasts and between her legs. She grew at once tense and rigid; her grip on his cock became at the same time uncomfortable and arousing. He withdrew his hands, contenting himself with petting her upper thigh with his left hand and covering her right hand with his, clasping it from behind.

She, for her part, stared at his cock and at her own

hand, engaged in what to her must have been quite an unthinkable act, stared with an odd mixture of fascination and confused dismay, as if she found herself in a disturbing dream from which she was unable to awake.

To his surprise, Sol found Jana's discomfort and embarrassment intensely arousing. He had always opted for uninhibited, even enthusiastic companionship from women, both in his personal relationships (all in the past now, sadly) and when choosing from one of those catalogs. How strange at his age to discover a small dark corner of kink in his own libido. He wondered what its limits were. He did not think he would find it arousing in the least to actually rape Jana, but this reluctance of hers, this almost immature shyness, this game of pushing her toward some edge, this testing of her boundaries he found quite exciting.

And a good thing, too, he mused. Because it was the only thing keeping him hard at the moment. Jana was as inept at masturbating a man – at masturbating Sol at least – as she was adept at masturbating herself.

"Haven't you ever done this before?" Sol asked not unkindly.

Jana shook her head while she continued to mechanically move her hand up and down.

"Not even with your boyfriend?"

At this Jana broke into a low sob. "Don't," she said, "please don't make me talk about him while we're...while I'm...doing this!"

"It's okay," Sol said, going limp; "you can stop for a while."

Jana covered her face with both hands and wept almost silently.

**

Sol paced. Three steps and then the awkward half-step. He paced nude for several minutes but then a certain self-consciousness about his body began to invade his thoughts, and he snatched his flight suit from the floor and put it on.

He resumed pacing.

It was not that he was grossly fat or even out of shape. He kept himself pretty trim. Over the years he had come to see that a fit, powerful body made the mind that much more fit and powerful. There was really no separation of the mind and the body: those two seemingly incongruous human elements were intertwined on some fundamental level. He often found this to be particularly true in his dealmaking. It wasn't always enough to outthink the other guy; there were times when it came down to who brought the most intimidating physical presence to a meeting. And it wasn't just about height or bulk of muscle. Sol was no more than on the low fringe of average in either area. It was about presence, about self-assurance, about how one carried oneself: size and fitness and sharpness of mind were all elements of the thing – but no one of those elements alone, nor all three elements together, was the thing itself.

What made Sol self-conscious now was his age – even his apparent age. It occurred to him that Jana, twenty-one year-old Jana, looked upon Sol's apparent thirty-somethingness as being prohibitively old. She pined for her young boyfriend. Human souls, if they existed, might be incomprehensibly old, as old as creation itself, but a young woman's soulmate needed to be no more than five or six years older than she was in bodily appearance.

And what if Jana could see past the mask of Sol's body? What if intuition (or perhaps an old-fashioned google search) gave her glimpses of Sol's real age? She would see him as not just prohibitively old but as impossibly old.

If she had any sort of intuitive sight on the age question, he thought it best not to parade around in front of her stark naked.

But too old for what, goddammit! He wasn't proposing they spend a lifetime together, just eight days of uninhibited carnal entanglement. Not even eight days — the initial high-g blackout period had consumed the better part of twenty-four hours and the de-acceleration period at the end of the trip would do the same.

Jana chose that moment to ask if she, too, could put on her flight suit.

"No!" Sol snapped. "Clean up the wine packages. Then, I suppose, we ought to think about having something to eat."

He had to show her the narrow chute where trash was deposited so that it existed no longer as payload but instead was incinerated as fuel. Jana dumped the empty wine containers down the chute.

"Should I put my jumpsuit and underwear in as well?" she asked coldly.

They gazed at each other, eye to eye, for a long time.

Sol said, "Don't get passive-aggressive on me, baby; it doesn't become you and it won't bring out the best in me, I promise."

Then: "No, don't throw any of your clothes down the chute. It was very sexy when you stripped earlier. I may want you to do that again."

"Yes, sir," Jana said, but she continued to challenge him with her eyes.

**

She knew where the food and drinks were stowed: in lockers under the circular couch. The flight technicians had oriented her to that extent at least.

She brought out two vacuum-sealed packages: "poached salmon and gourmet grilled vegetables." She inserted them into a slot near the forward bulkhead. The slot was the smaller of the two marked "kitchen." Six minutes later, two steaming plates emerged from the lower, larger slot. The plates were impossibly thin but remarkably rigid in spite of the fact that they were made of a nearly weightless material that seemed to be a cross between plastic and paper. The silverware was made of the same material.

There was a narrow break in the circular couch so that a person could move from the main area of the cabin to the "kitchen" and the bathroom. An even narrower table could be made to pivot by an ingenious system from under one end of the couch so that two people sitting on either side of the break could have the table between them. It would not have been out of place, Sol thought, in one of those old-timey pop-up campers. His grandfather had owned one, had once taken Sol on an overnight fishing trip with it into the wilds of upstate New York. *Wow*, Sol thought, *that's going way back; I couldn't have been older than seven or eight.* He almost mentioned it now to Jana: the camper, the fishing trip, his grandfather, how much like the untamed wilderness upstate New York seemed, how wonderful and new everything in the world seemed back then: small talk over a meal – but he restrained himself. On the trip, in the camper at night, his grandfather had told stories of his own childhood, events that had happened impossibly long ago. Unconsciously,

Sol did not want to be that person in the present moment.

He had told Jana to get more wine but she had brought only a single package and set it by his plate. She sat on her side of the narrow table, hunching as low as possible, trying to hide her breasts. She picked at a gourmet grilled chunk of zucchini. She was miserable and self-conscious.

"All right, all right," Sol relented; "go put your clothes on already."

Jana did not hesitate but she did not rush either. Sol watched her step into her panties and work them up her legs, watched her install and position the skin-toned bra, watched as she slowly, slowly wriggled herself into her flight suit. She kept her face turned away from him but he could tell that she knew he was watching. She moved with a ponderous sort of grace, as if purposefully giving him something to look at, not posing for him precisely but trying nonetheless to deliver some level of pleasure given the existence of their agreement. Or, maybe he was reading too much into it. Maybe the wine affected her more than it did him. Maybe she was going slow because her head was swimming. Sol couldn't be sure what to make of it but he decided to take it as a good sign, as a display of willingness on her part to perform as per their contract.

She toed on her flip-flops and returned to the table. She gave him a shy smile, nothing more. Sol had hoped for a significant look, a "did you like that?" kind of look but her eyes were innocent and perhaps slightly blank.

He encouraged her to eat, and she ate more heartily now. He encouraged her to get more wine for herself but she demurred. The food was quite good; Sol's instruction as to food had been to spare no expense, and, judging by this one meal, his suppliers had delivered value for every dollar. The wine, of course, was as excellent as Mars could produce: it came from Sol's own premier vineyard.

He invited her to tell him about herself. Where was she from? What were her interests? What were the details of how she wound up on Mars?

She came from Kansas. From a little crossroads town in eastern Kansas called Blue Mound.

"From Kansas? Seriously?"

"Yes, from Kansas," Jana said darkly and defensively.

Sol grinned.

"What's wrong with coming from Kansas?"

"Nothing, nothing," Sol insisted. "It just feels like maybe there's a connection with Dorothy in *The Wizard of Oz*: 'there's no place like home, there's no place like home'."

Jana's frown slowly unclouded, became almost a smile. "Okay, I guess I can see that," she said.

Sol's heart gave a sudden small leap. A younger Sol, in pursuit of a woman, would not have paused to study the sensation, would simply have moved in the indicated direction. The current Sol, possessed still by the same instinct to pounce without hesitation, could pause nevertheless and study. He felt a remarkable surge of energy simply by contemplating the fact that he and Jana had between them this cultural point of connection: the 1939 movie classic *The Wizard of Oz*. (There was an even older book, he was aware – but who read books?) It had been a point of connection between Sol and his parents, between Sol and his grandparents, between his grandparents and their parents it went so far back. It had been a point of connection between Sol and his own kids and their kids, and now it was a bridge between Sol and Jana, a member more or less of the generation the same age as his many grandchildren.

Jana mused, "Am I traveling back to Kansas with the Lion, the Tinman or the Scarecrow? Or am I in the presence of the Wizard himself?"

"You're with Toto," Sol shot back: "the little dog always looking up Dorothy's skirt."

Jana blushed but could not completely repress a subversive smile.

They ate in companionable silence. Sol finished his wine and asked if she would share one more with him. Jana agreed. She retrieved a packet of wine from the food locker, a shiraz this time. They passed it back and forth.

"This is different from the other wine," Jana observed.

With his eyes and a motion of his hand, Sol invited her to elaborate.

"It's not as deep or earthy or something and, I don't know, it's more spicy." She hastened to add, "But it's good: I don't mean to say it isn't good!"

"Bravo," Sol said. "You have an excellent palate for wine."

Jana ate all her vegetables and most of her salmon. Sol finished the salmon for her: from childhood he had been taught not to let good food go to waste. Jana finished the wine.

"Let's take a walk," Sol urged.

Jana was puzzled.

Sol said, "I'll show you."

He led her to the Spartan lavatory.

Jana grew immediately distrustful. "I don't understand, where are you taking me?" she asked, nearly pleading, pulling away as they entered the narrow space.

"Watch this," Sol said, flipping a switch on the wall.

The lights dimmed as the plumbing fixtures trundled out of sight, and suddenly they were standing on a wide, bright, sun-drenched, Earthly beach. On their left were sand dunes and wind-tossed sea grasses; on their right was a glittering, calm ocean, an intricate kaleidoscope of greens and blues and grays, crosshatched by irregular, transitory, undulating lines of foamy wave tops. Directly before them the wide, winding, sandy beach stretched on into a hazy infinity. Sandpipers hurried up and down the shingle, pecking incessantly, alternately chasing and being chased by the surf. Gulls quipped and cawed, circling near and far; some gulls, unseen, could only be heard behind them; others, practically overhead, cast fleeting shadows across the bodies of Sol and Jana. The sun was near the top of an almost cloudless sky of stunning blue, and there was a powerful sea breeze. The breeze could hardly do more than ruffle Sol's close-cropped hair, but Jana had to keep brushing wind-battered locks out of her landward eye.

"Let's walk," Sol said.

Jana looked at him uncertainly.

Had she not heard him over the wind and the subdued roar of the surf? Or did she still understand, correctly, despite the evidence of her senses, that she was standing inside an impossibly small space, a space where there was no room to walk? It didn't matter. Sol did not feel like repeating himself, did not feel like explaining. He took her arm and, pulling her with him, strode ahead.

Jana put her unencumbered hand up, afraid of bumping into the wall she knew was just before them. But they never came to the wall. Instead, they strolled into the seaside landscape, and the landscape shifted around them as their point of view flowed forward.

"This is incredible!" Jana enthused after a quarter

mile or so, hugging his arm. "I've never experienced anything like it. How is it possible?"

"Holographics," Sol said. He couldn't tell if Jana had heard him or, hearing, had understood. She was glancing rapidly all around her. He started to explain about the floor being a somewhat improved treadmill when she suddenly pulled her arm free of his and bolted forward then turned sharply into the dunes. Jana's abrupt movement caused Sol to lose his balance and he tumbled backward and crashed against a wall of the lavatory. Jana ran with abandon and the landscape rushed past them, but she could not separate herself from Sol who, sitting on the ground, glided along beside her. Sol was lightly jostled occasionally by the unevenness of the ground but never enough to really hurt: the HyperWorld™ was programmed to spare human tissue over and above any concerns for verisimilitude.

Sol watched Jana's fit, shapely legs, her graceful, animal strides. He had the urge to reach out and grasp one of her ankles, to bring her down in a heap. A lion dropping a gazelle. Instead, he said in a loud, plaintive voice, "What do you think you're doing?"

Jana gave a horrified gasp to find Sol so close. She threw a desperate glance over her shoulder but did not see him.

"Down here," Sol said, waving his hand.

Jana glanced downward and, gasping again, got tangled up in her own feet. She fell face first into the sand.

They were back in the main cabin. Sol had scraped an elbow when he fell against the lavatory wall, and he was swabbing it with an antibacterial wipe.

"Did you think we were back on Earth?" he asked

crossly.

"No, I knew we couldn't be back so soon."

Sol pondered a moment and then he said: "You've never experienced a HyperWorld™ device before, have you? Not even one of these limited capacity models. That's it, isn't it?"

Jana sulked on a far corner of the couch, a red patch on her right cheek, and made no reply.

Sol said, "Okay, so you knew it wasn't really Earth, but still you thought you could hide out in that great, wide world inside the bathroom until we landed, didn't you?"

Jana would not look him in the eye.

Sol said in a wounded voice, "I thought we were trying to negotiate the terms of a contract in good faith." He wasn't sure himself how much he was truly wounded and how much it was just one more negotiator's ploy. "I was willing to consider something less than full performance under the contract on your part, but clearly your aim is to renege at any opportunity."

Jana glanced at him for an instant, her eyes at once defiant and contrite. She seemed on the verge of making some reply but no words escaped her.

"I'm tired," Sol said. "I need to sleep. Get me two white pills. We'll discuss the HyperWorld™ incident further tomorrow."

Jana obediently fetched two pills.

"Get one for yourself, if you want to," Sol said; "it will knock you right out, I guarantee."

Jana took no white pill for herself.

In times of stress, the white pills were a sure portal into sleep. Sol had been an intermittent insomniac his whole life, and the white pills were a far cry from the knockout drugs that he remembered from decades ago. The old drugs would put you under, sure enough, but you'd emerge next morning from a kind of dreamless oblivion, still partially drugged, still exhausted. The white pills brought true, restful sleep, fostered dreams in abundance: organic dreams, restorative dreams, not oblivion and not the psychedelics or paranoid frenzies that certain other drugs often inflicted.

Even now, with all the stress of hurtling between worlds in a living space hardly larger than a coffin, the white pills did not fail him. One pleasant, slow-moving, intricate dream followed on another. Each held his attention fully and each passed out of his memory completely when succeeded by the next.

Until he found himself in a shadowy replica of the diminutive cabin of the *Speedy*. He was pacing, looking for something. No, not something…someone. The girl. Jana. He was looking for Jana. She was missing. But where could she have gone? There was nowhere to go, no way out until they reached Earth. He found her in the bathroom, hiding. Was she hiding? Found her at any rate staring at herself in the mirror above the tiny sink. Her flight suit lay in a heap around her ankles. He grasped her by the wrist and pulled her into the main cabin.

He heard himself grumbling at her. "Thought you could just run out and leave Sol Vincente looking like a fool, did you?" And: "No one beats Sol Vincente in a business deal! No one, you understand?!" These were the things he intended to say. In his dream, his grumbling became an incoherent growling.

He sat on the circular couch and pulled her across his knee, positioning her for a spanking. She resisted him hardly at all. The first contact of his hand with her upturned ass was shocking to him in its intensity and its clarity, as events often are in a dream. The sharp, hard crack; the arch of her back; the sting in his hand; the cratering of the cheek he had struck, the rebound to perfect roundness, the slowly subsiding after-ripples. His hand rose and fell. At some point he dragged her white panties down to her knees; she tried to interfere and he pinned her wrist to the small of her back and continued to spank her until her ass glowed a deep Martian red.

Sol woke exquisitely refreshed. He yawned and stretched. Even the cramped space, the lowering ceiling could not, for the moment, suppress his contentment. He was flat on his back, square in the middle of the widened and specially padded place on the circular couch that approximated the dimensions of a queen-sized bed. He glanced to either side of him: Jana was not there.

He found her asleep on a curve of the couch furthest from him. She was rolled into a protective ball: her knees tucked up close to her chest, her arms shielding her head. She seemed to be huddling inside her flight suit as if she were cold. There was one blanket on board and Sol had slept under it. A blanket on such a flight was an unheard of luxury. There was no need: the cabin temperature could be controlled to within a fraction of a degree. But Sol had insisted: a blanket could be a very comforting thing. The blanket they had shipped was as sheer as the wing of a butterfly, as light as air itself. Sol doubled it and placed it gently around Jana's sleeping form.

He heated a pouch of black coffee, French roast, and drank it in small sips. The ship's clock was still on Mars time, and Sol noted that back on Mars in the vicinity of Hellas Planitia it was a few minutes past eight in the morning. Counting the day they boarded as day one, it was the third day of the flight – five days and a few hours to go.

Many Martian settlers claimed to have trouble adjusting to Mars time. It was such a common complaint that it had become something of a planetary conversational cliché. People couldn't very well discuss the weather on arid Mars, where the forecast always called for strong sunshine and the thin skies were either clear or dusty, so they talked about the difficulty of adjusting to the Martian day. Sol had never had a problem with it. The Martian day, the time it took Mars to spin around once on its axis, measured in Earth time, was twenty-four hours, thirty-seven minutes and about twenty seconds. Big deal. Sol had always felt back on Earth that the days were too short, anyway. Who in their right mind would complain about living on a planet where the clocks were set to tick a little slower? So that you still had the old, familiar twenty-four hour day, you still seemingly had sixty minutes to the hour, but the slower-ticking clocks were cunningly adding about one and a half minutes to each hour, so that from one day to the next when the clocks struck noon the sun stayed at the top of the sky. Sol had once started to figure out what his real age was in Martian days; that is to say, in Martian rotations. But as he worked the numbers in his head he saw that the difference would be slight and so he never completed the calculation. What was the point? In real years he was old on Earth and he was old on Mars. Too bad. On the other hand, if one considered the actual Martian year, the length of time it took Mars to make a single revolution around the sun…

Jana stirred.

Sol went back to the kitchen to heat up another pouch of coffee.

They passed each other, she on her way to the bathroom, he moving toward the place on the circular couch where his notepad had been left. Their eyes met briefly. Sol caught a complex glimpse of accusation and acquiescence. It startled him. And at the same moment it caused him to notice that the hand he had spanked her with in his dream was ruddy and slightly swollen. Had he actually spanked her?

He putzed around on his notepad for a while but it hardly offered any distraction. Back on Mars, he would have used his notepad or some other electronic device to catch up on local, Martian news or to review reports from Earth (from four to twenty-four minutes delayed depending on the relative positions of the two planets in their respective orbits around the sun) or, most commonly, to study the constantly fluctuating values of his vast holdings and investments across two worlds. For reasons Sol did not fully understand, none of that was possible during an eight-day transit. To move at such speed, the ship needed to create some kind of energy barrier around itself, otherwise a collision with even a pebble-sized particle could be catastrophic; and the barrier cut off all communication with the outside world. One more reason to feel claustrophobic, as far as Sol was concerned.

Jana's contract called for her to provide not only sexual services but domestic services as well. She set about fulfilling the domestic portion of her contract with reserved efficiency. She made a quick inventory of the food pouches. She announced to Sol what his choices were from among the pouches that seemed like breakfast food. Sol chose scrambled eggs and toast along with hashbrowns. Jana ate a small portion of cinnamon flavored oatmeal. They hardly spoke during the meal. At one point, Sol asked, "Don't you want any coffee?" Jana replied that she didn't drink coffee.

"How about tea?"

Jana reported that there didn't seem to be any tea on board.

"What is there?" Sol asked.

"Pretty much it's red wine and coffee."

"My two favorite drinks," Sol said.

After breakfast, Jana deposited the dishes into the appropriate slot, stowed away the blanket Sol had covered her with, straightened out the cushions at the wide portion of the couch where Sol had slept, and positioned herself on the circular couch as far from Sol as she could be. Sol soon tired of his notepad, of his essentially useless notepad: for him the thing was a communication tool or nothing at all.

"I'm going to take a shower," Sol said. "Why don't you join me?"

A shower on board the *Speedy* did not involve actual water. Water was heavy and expensive to transport. A shower on board the *Speedy* involved innumerable intricately aimed micro-lasers cleansing a person's every surface, every crevice, skin and hair, while holographic water flowed from a holographic shower head. The bottle of shampoo, the soap in the soap dish were holograms, too.

It was all very convincing, however, and Sol lathered and scrubbed himself vigorously amidst the billowing clouds of holographic steam.

Sol noticed that he had no feelings of claustrophobia while in the shower. He supposed that he was accustomed to showers not being very roomy. Also, it was somehow comforting to know that he could step out into the larger space of the bathroom and then again into the larger space of the cabin; what was so disconcerting about the cabin was that there was no larger space to escape to from there.

Jana appeared just as Sol was beginning to give up hope that she would. She stepped shyly into the shower enclosure, naked. It was a cramped space, so tight that two people could not occupy it together without touching. That was fine by Sol. But Jana attempted to keep some miniscule distance between them.

Sol tried to turn her toward the holographic spray of water but it was too hot for her. Sol dialed down the temperature.

Water cascaded through her hair. She closed her eyes and lifted her face and water streamed over her shoulders and across her breasts. She lost her balance momentarily, tipping backward; she put out her hands and immediately they came into contact with Sol's lean midsection; Sol, misunderstanding, grasped her shoulders and pulled her toward him; she tensed and in a flash Sol got it and released her.

When she opened her eyes again Jana gave him a smile. Not the open, inviting smile Sol might have hoped for. More of a brave, resigned smile, almost forlorn. But a smile nonetheless.

Sol bumped the shower door open with his rear end and stood partway out of the stall so as to create a bit more space between him and Jana. Sol turned her once then twice so that her whole body glistened with a perfect imitation of water.

"We're flooding the bathroom floor," Jana observed. Sol shrugged and shampooed her hair.

Her hair was thin and straight and hung partway down her back, several inches longer than shoulder length, longer than in her catalog photos, a mix of colors: brown sugar and golden honey. The holographic water made the brown parts darker and the streaks of honey lighter. He tipped her head back and lathered her carefully so as not to get any suds in her eyes. He rinsed her in the same manner, starting from the crown of her forehead and working his way to the tips of her hair.

He soaped her next, working up a lather with his hands, delicately finger painting her face with soap bubbles, careful around her eyes, then turning her, massaging her neck, her shoulders, her arms all the way down to her fingertips, her hips and her sides all the way up again to under her arms, then her back starting just below her shoulders and working his way downward until he was gently fondling her ass. He slipped a finger in between her cheeks and soaped her asshole. She shivered or shuddered, he wasn't sure which.

He played with her ass for a while longer then he turned her around. As he worked up a new lather they gazed directly into each other's eyes. Jana's gaze was unflinching and impenetrable. It called to mind images Sol had seen ages ago, lifetimes ago, at the Uffizi back on Earth in Florence. The face of a martyr, he thought, at the moment when immolation verges into transcendence. What did it mean? Instinct told him that his slow, soapy exploration of her body was not altogether unpleasant for Jana. He was perfectly well aware of how fallible a man's instinct could be in such situations. But Sol Vincente was not a man to distrust his instinct.

He touched her gently on either side of her neck, spread soap bubbles across her lightly freckled chest. Her gaze fell at the first tenuous contact between his hands and her exquisite, compact breasts. As he caressed her, her naturally brownish areola began to glow a subtle pink, not unlike the changing hues of the Martian sunrise. Her brow clouded deeper and deeper as her nipples became more and more erect. He kissed each one with a kind of carnal reverence. His massaging hands moved to her belly of their own accord, without his knowledge – without hers as well, he suspected – but, when his fingertips began to brush against her modest growth of pubic hair, both he and she became acutely aware of the event.

Sol had been crouching to kiss Jana's breasts. Now he knelt before her, his feet fully out of the shower enclosure. One hand went between her legs, the other curved around the small of her back and pulled her to him. He kissed her lower and lower on her belly until he was kissing her diminutive triangle of pubic hair. She pushed feebly against his shoulders and he heard her voice softly through the fall of the water saying, "Oh." And then again, "Oh!"

He pushed her backward a few inches, until her shoulders were against the wall of the shower stall. In a real shower, the water would have been shooting somewhat past them, past her at least. But in the *Speedy's* waterless, weight-saving rendition of a shower, the computer-generated, holographic water-image followed the bather or bathers wherever he or she or they happened to be, so that the water still cascaded straight down upon the two of them.

Sol was therefore hindered in his attempt to glance up and catch Jana's eye. *Was she enjoying this? Was he taking things too far, too fast?*

He sent both his arms between her legs and, raising them, picked her up. He positioned her so that her thighs draped across his shoulders; her heels bumped against the middle of his back; her glistening vagina lay wide open directly in front of his eyes. He played a forefinger over the lips of her vagina, delicately moving them aside to more fully reveal her sex and particularly her rose-red clitoris. He touched her clit with the utmost tenderness, moving his finger in slow, dreamy circles.

Jana smelled, as every woman did, of the ocean, of the Earthly ocean. Intermixed was her own personal scent, her own *saveur*. He had caught hints of it last night when she masturbated herself. He caught more than hints of it now, and it excised him deeply.

He planted a first kiss on her vagina. His tongue so wanted to dart inside and fully taste her. But he restrained himself. He nuzzled her clit with his lips, moving at first up and down and then, more forcefully, side to side. Jana's suppressed gasps and moans were nevertheless easily heard above the hiss of the shower.

She came with the same uncomplicated readiness that she had evinced the night before. But now with surprisingly more passion. She clasped his hair, alternately kneading and pulling; she squeezed his head so tight between her thighs that he thought his ears would be crushed; she writhed upon his shoulders, the heels of her feet at times drumming his back. She came in waves, in sweetly convulsive waves, with sometimes a brief ebb between convulsions, but often with one tumultuous wave piling in on top of another, creating a confused, ecstatic crescendo.

At last the ebbs became longer and more numerous. During one of these ebbs, he shifted away from her clit and, nuzzling and kissing her squarely on her vagina, entered her with his tongue. Her outer body grew slightly tense but inside she was warm and overflowing with vaginal juices. He moved his tongue delicately up and down, tasting her fully.

He had never noticed this in a woman before but Jana tasted sweeter near to what Sol thought of as the top of her vagina, close to her clitoris, almost like some tropical fruit, reminiscent of mango or guava but subtly different; she tasted saltier and more bitter as his tongue moved downward, like clay, like earth and ocean; and, when he thrust his tongue straight into her, he thought he detected hints of almond or perhaps hazelnut as well as overripe blackberry.

Inwardly, momentarily, he mocked himself: *Sol Vincente, connoisseur of twat.*

But the mocking only served to forestall a question he could not avoid: *Had this richness of experience always been available to him? Had he utterly missed it until now?*

Sol was too involved in the moment to be distracted by any interior question, and he filed his thoughts away for later examination, while his tongue and lips carried on with the pleasures of the moment.

His nose, too. Most decidedly his nose: Sol found that the rich, deep scent of her was intertwined with the complexities of how she tasted, that he could not fully experience one without the other. Also, while his tongue explored deeper and deeper, his nose by happy circumstance nuzzled her clit, setting off in Jana a new series of slow orgasms.

It ended of its own accord. One moment he was ravishing her with his mouth, the next her legs were off his shoulders and he was quietly soaping her crotch, her legs, her feet, completing the task of washing her.

When he stood, the tip of his more than semi-erect penis nudged between her legs. Jana tried to back away but there was no room for retreat. She was confused, conflicted: that was plain to see on her sweet ingenuous face. To Sol it seemed that he could read her thoughts as effortlessly as if she were speaking out loud. She had taken pleasure from the intimate touch of a man who was not her soulmate and so there was guilt. There was an inclination to be outraged: this man had all but ordered her into the shower with him, had taken obscene liberties with her that she had never asked for or consented to: yet she was clearly uncertain about how far she could claim to be outraged, given the contract for services that existed between them: uncertain, too, about how far she actually did feel outraged, recalling her pleasure. She struggled to resolve this circular, multi-sided debate. Sol watched and waited, interested to see if she could find the maturity or depth or pliancy or whatever it took to resolve the issues in her mind. She did not. As far as Sol could see, she did not; instead, she dealt with the unresolved debate, as people typically did, by leaving it unresolved and simply allowing her mind to move on to another topic.

The other topic was him, Sol. She noticed him watching her and she now returned his gaze, his attention. She did it almost dutifully, it seemed to Sol. As if she felt the least she could do as a space companion was not to ignore the person whose companion she was supposed to be, especially given the circumstance that they stood inches apart and fully unclothed in a steaming shower.

Jana's frank blue eyes stared directly into his. He still had the earthy, salty taste of her in his mouth and he felt the urge to kiss her, to give her as a gift a taste of herself. But he wanted the next move to be hers. She seemed to read that in him and he watched her working out in her mind what the expected next move must be. She gulped and, with a look of pitiable dread, took up the shampoo bottle and began to lather Sol's hair. When she was done with his hair she followed Sol's routine precisely, soaping his face, then working her way down his body. Her hands were tense, unsoothing; her face took on a look of stoney resignation. By the time she finally crouched before him, bringing her face to the level of his cock, and allowed her fingers to touch the edges of his dark mass of pubic hair, reluctantly as if it were something diseased, Sol had gone quite limp. Using her hands, Jana made a half-hearted and fumbling attempt to revive him. But it was no use. Sol could feel no excitement, no positive energy between them anymore. He took her gently by the shoulders and urged her to a standing position. He looked at her beautiful, lithe, young body, letting his eyes play slowly down then up again over every inch of her. He could not bear to do more than glance at her face. He sighed and left the shower.

He lingered at the narrow mirror above the equally narrow sink. He needed a shave but he would come back for that later, after Jana had left the bathroom. His hair was too short to need combing, even after having been shampooed. Of course, it was perfectly dry since it had never been more than holographically wet. Sol looked briefly into his own gray, hawkish eyes. The old, familiar, entrepreneurial hunger was still in them but there was a sadness, a weariness also that made him turn swiftly away.

Jana asked sheepishly about how to turn off the shower.

"Just step out," Sol said.

Sol had left the tiny door to the shower ajar, and Jana now pulled it partway shut and peeked around the edge. She seemed to be looking for something but Sol couldn't figure out what.

"Aren't there any towels?" she asked.

"No need," Sol said. Then, again, "Just step out."

Jana stepped partway out. She seemed to be trying to keep the shower door between herself and Sol. Sol found her relentless modesty to be both childish and silly, given the situation they were in. Part of him was annoyed by it, but more than anything else it deepened his gloom. He made use of a small container of mouthwash to remove the taste of her from his mouth. In the corner of his eye, he could see her marveling at her suddenly dry skin and hair and at the dry floor. He removed his flight suit from the niche in the wall where he had left it to be freshened. He left her alone in the bathroom without explanation.

Unless altered by its occupants, the cabin's lights were programmed to mimic a typical Martian day in the latitude of Hellas Planitia: an abrupt sunrise at about 7:30, steady sunshine until perhaps 2:00 in the afternoon, then a perceptible dimming to mark the usual dust storms that rose in the heat of the day especially during spring and summer, then renewed bright sunshine for perhaps an hour before the lingering sunset which began at about 6:30 in the evening and faded into relative darkness until the following dawn. Left to themselves, the cabin lights did not go entirely dark at "night." Rather, they emitted a persistent glow somewhat similar to the intense starshine that penetrated the thin Martian atmosphere, a quantity of light sufficient to cautiously move about in once one's eyes were accustomed to it.

Sol spent the better part of that "day" moping, brooding, pacing. He paced in brief spells. He couldn't bear to do more. The pacing reminded him of how little room there was and tended to panic him. But sitting was almost as bad. Once at about midday he allowed himself a single blue pill. He felt he had to limit his intake of the psychoactive drug this early in the trip. Alcohol, too, for that matter. Hell, they were barely more than forty-eight hours out, whether one counted in Earth hours or Mars hours. But that thought sent a new wave of panic through him, and he very nearly took a second pill, very nearly dove into the wine locker. The hours of entombment stretched before him like an eternity.

While Sol brooded, Jana moved about the cabin on tiptoe searching for domestic chores to perform. She made a thorough inventory of all the lockers under the couch. She discovered an entire locker, which she must have overlooked earlier, full of beverages other than red wine and coffee. There was a variety of hard liquor and liqueurs, as well as fruit drinks, soft drinks, diet and regular, even a couple of packages marked "iced tea, green" lemon and mint. She told Sol of her discovery, calling him "Mr. Vincente," but Sol merely glanced at her then looked away.

What had distressed him in the shower was Jana's lack of generosity. What he perceived to be her lack of generosity. She was willing to receive pleasure but she felt sullied or demeaned somehow when she was called upon to give pleasure. She could not even allow him the pleasure of looking at her lithe, young body without ruining the fun by being so obviously uncomfortable when her clothes were off.

Shortly after he took the blue pill, Jana suggested they eat lunch. Sol mumbled something about not being hungry.

"You should probably eat if you're going to take those pills," Jana said. Sol gave her a cold look and she added, "Sir."

Sol went back to pacing, his step becoming more strident with every turn.

Suddenly, he wheeled on her.

"I'm setting some ground rules," he seethed. "I call

you Jana, you call me Sol, got it? I just ate your pussy in the shower and, as far as I could tell, you loved it, so knock off the 'Mr. Vincente' crap, okay? We're on first names now, even if there's still a big disagreement between us.

"And if you ever call me 'sir' again, I'll...I'll do to you what I dreamed about doing to you last night."

Let her wonder what that might be, Sol thought: her imagination was sure to conjure up something far worse than a silly spanking.

Jana stood at attention, head bowed, hands clasped before her. "Yes...um, Sol," she murmured.

Sol regarded her, trying to figure her out, finding little success. Was she blushing?

"Go ahead and fix lunch," Sol ordered with more show of annoyance than he felt. The dealmaker in him sensed he had gained some kind of upper hand with his outburst and he did not want to lose it. Inwardly he reasoned: if she's talking about lunch she must be hungry herself.

She began to ask about his preferences but he cut her off. "Just make it happen," he told her.

She served them both an exquisite French concoction that Sol could not have named but that his palate would not soon forget. She served them both, too, containers of red wine, the brunello. Sol only occasionally drank wine with lunch, more usually in the evening with dinner. But if Jana was game, so was he.

He wasn't quite finished with the wine he was drinking when she brought him another.

"I'll have a second if you will," Sol said.

Jana's wine container was still a quarter full.

"I can't keep up with you," she pleaded and paused, releasing a small, nearly silent burp, then added: "Sol."

Sol said, "You're not trying hard enough. Jana."

Jana dutifully sipped at her wine. When she finished she said, "Oh my, my head's swimming. That's all for me. But you have another."

"Let's split it," Sol suggested.

"I couldn't," Jana said. "Really."

Sol said, "You just need to walk off the first one. Tell you what, let's go for a walk together and we'll split this one along the way."

Jana said, "I don't want to walk on that beach again, Sol. It will make me remember how badly I acted."

"Okay," Sol said, "we'll walk someplace else. I know a really cool place in San Francisco that I bet is in the HyperWorld™ database. Ever been to San Francisco?"

"Never," Jana said.

"Let's go, then."

While Sol fiddled with the settings on the HyperWorld™ Jana cleared the dishes and stowed the tiny fold-out table. She came to him carrying the new wine packet and two blue pills.

"Now that you've eaten, it won't hurt to take one more," Jana said, offering him a pill. "And I'll bring along an extra on our walk just in case."

"I'm good," Sol said.

"But why wait until you're starting to panic? Why not keep ahead of it? It must be terrible to not like small spaces and to be so completely stuck in *such* a small space for so long. I don't know how you stand it."

Sol considered taking the pill. Jana's concern was so sincere. Why *not* keep ahead of the panic? He was a little buzzed himself from the lunchtime wine and the one pill he had already taken. But something held him back.

"Tell you what," he said, "I'll take one while we're walking, if I feel the need. But in any case I'll take at least one before we come back to our 'small space,' as you call it. Thanks for being so considerate."

Jana gave him a beaming smile.

One at a time, first Jana then Sol, they stepped through the narrow door of the lavatory onto the brilliantly lit, wind-tossed pedestrian walkway of the Golden Gate Bridge.

There was no car traffic at all. Sol had programmed it out. On the real bridge, car traffic was noisy and smelly and, of course, confined pedestrians to the rather narrow concrete walkway. Sol did not want any feeling of confinement while in the HyperWorld™. There was a scattering of other pedestrians: a few miniature figures far ahead on the walkway, a few others closer by, meandering across the deserted highway lanes. Sol and Jana waved to a young married couple whose three kids — boys: triplets, or perhaps a pair of twins and an undersized older brother — raced back and forth from one side of the roadbed to the other pretending to be airplanes, their arms outstretched, their mouths in odd, happy grimaces making droning engine sounds.

The day was transcendentally clear: no hint at all of the usual Bay Area fog. Sol and Jana were on the San Francisco side of the bridge; the wild, sparse hills of Marin County loomed far ahead. San Francisco itself glittered like a white diamond to their right. Sol took Jana's arm and led her forward over the dizzying expanse. He pointed out Alcatraz Island, the New Coit Tower (and the remains of the old one), the Transamerica Pyramid, glimpses of Fisherman's Wharf behind Alcatraz. Far below, on the bay side of the bridge, small sailing boats heeled in the strong wind; the Sausalito ferry cut a determined path through the choppy waters. To the left, on the ocean side, the water was tumultuous, rocky, dangerous. No small boats ventured out that way. And yet there was a dim line of minute boxy shapes on the far western horizon. Sol explained to Jana that those small shapes were actually transport ships of enormous dimensions.

"Oh," Jana gulped.

For the first time Sol noticed that Jana was looking somewhat peaked.

"What's the matter?" Sol bellowed over the wind.

"It's wonderful," Jana assured him. Her hands were shaking.

"Are you afraid of heights?" Sol shouted, slightly incredulous because heights exhilarated him.

"Yes. A little. Maybe," Jana answered in a weakening voice.

"C'mon," Sol said, and he leapt down onto the roadbed, pulling Jana along behind him, turning as he landed and catching her in his arms. Sol was pleasantly surprised at how well the limited-capacity HyperWorld™ handled the physics of such an abrupt, complex, dual-body movement.

The young married couple and their three kids had been walking toward the San Francisco side and were well behind them now, receding rapidly out of earshot. Before Sol and Jana the bridge loomed like a magnificent sculpture, as if its only purpose was to shape the endless blue of the sky within the flimsy, finite, paltry, man-made and yet somehow sufficient rust-red etchings of tower and cable. There was no angle of vision down from here: only forward and backward; side to side (somewhat obstructed by the bridge itself); and up up up. Jana seemed slightly more at ease but not completely.

Sol said, "If you're up high and you don't like it, the first rule, the only rule is: don't look down. My granddad taught me that a long time ago. He had a mild fear of heights and he figured I might, too, but I don't, never have."

Jana smiled bravely and marched forward.

Sol reveled in the clean salt air, the bright warm sunshine, the powerful wind. The bridge's vast web of cables could actually be heard humming, intricately resonating to the wind.

They were very far across the bridge, well beyond the midpoint before Sol noticed that Jana had not fully recovered, had not recovered much at all from her fear of heights.

"What's wrong?" Sol wanted to know, trying to tamp down his own exhilaration, trying to show genuine concern.

Jana refused to admit that anything was wrong.

"Here, have some of the wine we brought," she said, offering him the plastic container.

"*You* should have some of the wine," Sol said, pushing it away.

"I couldn't...really."

"Is it your stomach? Did the food upset your stomach?"

"Maybe, I'm not sure."

Sol peered at her.

"No," he said, "it's not your stomach: you're scared of something. Is it the height, still?"

"I don't think so."

"Are you scared of open spaces?"

Jana gave a weak laugh. "Not likely for a girl who grew up in Kansas."

"Oh right, I forgot about that...and the beach scene didn't bother you...but listen, whatever it is, we don't have to stay here: let's exit the program right now."

"But you're enjoying it so much and it's obviously doing you a lot of good."

"So what? We can exit this program and find one we both enjoy."

Jana patted his arm. "Let's stay right here. Only, please, let's turn around and head back toward where we started."

She put her arm in his and side by side they retraced their steps along the roadway. After a short distance, Jana, looking markedly better, said, "Let's go back up onto the pedestrian walk. The views are better up there."

"Okay," Sol said, "but the best way will probably be for the two of us to jump up together."

"Don't be silly," Jana said. "We can't jump that high. We have to climb up."

"I don't think this limited-capacity piece of junk can accommodate climbing," Sol said. "Just trust me on this: hold my hand and on three let's jump. Ready?...one, two, three!"

They jumped. The bridge seemed to drift downward at an unnaturally slow, dreamlike rate, until they were standing again on the pedestrian walkway.

"That was weird," Jana said.

Sol launched into a long tirade about the woeful inadequacies of the limited-capacity HyperWorld™, complete with a full description of the wonders of the deluxe model. When, finally, he exhausted the topic, it became immediately apparent to him that Jana had not attended to a single word: she was leaning on the outer rail of the bridge, gazing upon the capacious splendor of San Francisco Bay.

Behind them, the sun had moved perhaps halfway down the sky; the powerful winds had subsided to a confusion of erratic breezes. The bridge cast its shadow steadily further into the bay.

"It's magnificent," Jana said.

Sol put his arm around her waist, leaned against the rail, shared the view with her. There was no tension in her body now, no fear.

A sightseeing ferry passed under the bridge, headed back toward the city. Miniscule, smiling figures on the boat waved up at them; Sol and Jana waved back.

"Let me have that wine packet," Sol said, and he took a long sip and passed it back to Jana and she took a sip, too.

There was no one else on the bridge. They had it all to themselves. In fact, Sol and Jana had the whole vast holographic arena to themselves; tiny, waving sightseers notwithstanding: they being no more than pixels projected onto a nearby wall.

Sol turned Jana's face toward his and kissed her. She did not resist, but when he ended the kiss she turned away again.

Jana's hair swirled in front of her eyes. Sol gently captured the wayward strands, tucked them behind her ear, stroked the side of her face. "You never did tell me how you wound up on Mars," he said.

She glanced at him, glanced away. "Same way I wound up here, I guess," she shrugged by way of signaling disappointment in herself. "Not knowing what I was getting myself into, not reading the fine print."

"You came out as a Young Pioneer?"

"Exactly."

"And the Martian UAC right-to-work laws were news to you once you got here?...Or, I guess I should say 'there,' once you got to Mars?"

"The what?"

"The Under Any Contract right-to-work laws, the

laws that stipulate an employer and an employee, being 'free and equal individuals under the law,' may enter into any sort of contract, even one that involves ownership, if both parties so choose. Surely you must have heard of them?...they're commonly referred to as the Martian slave labor laws."

"Oh, those. Um-hmm, you're right, the first I heard of them was when I landed on Mars."

"But they're not exactly fine print: they're common knowledge back on Earth; in fact, they are the cause of much controversy between the two planets."

Jana sighed deeply, pretended to be entranced by the San Francisco skyline.

Sol said, "Okay, I get it, you weren't paying attention, you just signed up: what was it?...the spirit of adventure."

"Yes and no," Jana said wistfully.

"What does 'yes and no' mean?"

"Yes, I suppose it was the spirit of adventure; but on the other hand, no, it wasn't, at least not for me. It was my boyfriend: he was the one who wanted to go adventuring."

"Ah, the boychik," Sol said.

Jana waved a bothersome fly away from her face. She paid it no more attention than that but Sol, a dedicated HyperWorld™ user, sensed a sort of false verisimilitude: how would a fly find its way out onto the windy middle of the Golden Gate Bridge?

"But 'adventuring' is probably the wrong word," Jana said, turning toward him, thin strands of hair fluttering in front of her face. "It was more like he was just looking for a way to get ahead. There aren't many opportunities back on Earth for a couple of dumb kids like we were, just starting out without any advantages. Jason's parents have been working low-pay jobs their whole lives, no end in sight, and so have mine: maybe it isn't slavery, exactly, but it isn't their free choice either, I'm pretty certain of that. All you have to do is look into their faces.

"Jason thought we could find a better way. The Mars colonies being so new, he figured there had to be chances to get ahead out here...out there, wherever..."

"Why didn't you come out together?"

Jana just looked at him.

"Okay okay, I get it: too expensive, you only had the funds to send one. But why you and not him, the 'adventurer' or whatever he is?"

"That was the original plan. But then his mother got sick. It was almost certain she was going to die. We had already committed to one of us making the passage: we couldn't afford to lose all that money."

"Did she die, the boychik's mother?"

"I wish you would stop calling him that...I don't even know what it means."

"Ah it's just an old expression I picked up from my grandparents. But did she die?"

"I'm not sure."

"You're not *sure*? Doesn't he communicate, this...Jason?"

"Communication is not exactly easy when you're on two different planets!"

Sol took Jana's hand, the one holding the wine packet, and raised it until the narrow straw touched her lips. She sipped. Then he moved her hand to allow himself a drink. "Let's walk," he said.

Far overhead a commercial jetliner stole noiselessly across the sky, a white speck leaving a faint white wake.

"I hate riding in those things, too," Sol said: "Talk about confining!" Then, "I thought there was free email service between the two planets."

"There is."

"Okay, so what am I missing? How do you not know if his mother is alive?"

"Well, for one thing," Jana flounced, "since I landed on Mars my only access to a computer has been through the Young Pioneers' Charitable Outpost. Have you ever seen the lines in that place?"

Sol admitted that he had not. "But still..." he persisted.

"Of course I asked about Jason's mother every message I sent. Sometimes she would be better, sometimes worse. Then, at some point, he stopped responding about his mother. He still responds about other things but nothing about his mother."

Sol and Jana were approaching their starting point on the bridge. There seemed to be a tacit understanding between them that they would exit the program when they reached the starting point.

"Tell me something," Sol said. "Have his messages been getting shorter and spaced farther apart?"

Jana huffed. She slapped something small and light into Sol's left hand and the wine packet into his right. "You said you'd take another pill before we went back."

In the cabin of the *Speedy* "night" was fast approaching. Sol and Jana each separately brooded.

For Sol the shock of exiting the HyperWorld™ had been extreme: akin to waking up from a luminous, spacious fantasy into the smothering confines of a buried coffin. Perhaps the scale of the Golden Gate scenario had been a bit too drastic in comparison to the actual space in which Sol was confined. Perhaps a more moderate scenario would not result in this intense discomfort upon exiting. For instance, the beach scene had not done this to him; but then again at the end of the beach scene he had been distracted by Jana's silly attempt to flee. Sol's fear was that any scenario in the limited capacity HyperWorld™ would produce more harm than good: it might provide an hour or so of relief but the net result would be an ever increasing dread. But what were his options? Booze and pills? Well sure. But that couldn't be the answer every minute of every day.

He glanced at Jana who huddled opposite him, hugging herself as if she were cold, rocking slightly side to side, staring at the floor.

Jana was the option he had counted on. The only way to make the cramped space livable, survivable was to make it intimate and the only way to make it intimate was to share it very intimately with an attractive woman, with a woman who attracted him.

Was Jana either of those things anymore? Was she, in his eyes, an attractive woman? Was he attracted to her?

There was an important distinction here. He had met countless women in his life whom he had recognized as attractive, mostly for their looks but not always. Looks in a woman were of utmost importance to Sol; he freely admitted it: he was abjectly shallow in that regard. But looks alone were not enough. There had to be a certain level of intelligence, a strong sense of independence, a sense-of-humor, a vivacity. Without those qualities a woman, no matter how beautiful, might as well be a department store mannequin. On the other hand, much as Sol might admire intelligent, capable, funny, vivacious women, if they were not also physically striking he had no interest in them other than as fine Platonic company for the moment.

Jana was supple and slender, almost girlish, but curved just so in the delicate upsweep of her breasts, in the sweet roundness of her hips and ass, in the trim fitness of her legs, so that there was no mistaking her for a mere girl, and of course she had a pretty face: she was without doubt an attractive woman.

But was he attracted to her? Or, to put the question more bluntly, was Sol still interested in schlonging her?

The answer came immediately and urgently to his mind: yes!

The single pill he had taken upon exiting the HyperWorld™ was working to calm his thoughts without dulling them, and so he was able to understand his emphatic "yes" for what it was. He set about rephrasing the question: if you were back on Mars or, even better, home on Earth and you didn't need this nebbish to distract you from the current situation, would you have any interest in bonking her?

But the answer was there in his head before he could finish reformulating the question. Irrelevant!... you are *not* on Mars, you are *not* on Earth, you are here and now and you need what you planned on, you need what you paid for, you need her body as a distraction for your immediate wellbeing and survival!

Sol sighed. He wished that sometimes he could be more contemplative, less focused on the here and now. But his mind refused to work that way.

Okay, so he needed her (and perhaps wanted her) and had paid for her but the question still remained how was he going to get her, short of taking her by force.

Jana continued to slowly rock, side to side, and to stare vacantly at the floor. Sol went to the locker where the feather-weight blanket was stored. He pulled it out and draped it around Jana's shoulders. He searched for the wine container Jana had been carrying on the Golden Gate Bridge.

He found it on a ledge beside the bathroom door. He sipped from it, carried it to Jana, placed the straw before her lips. She didn't seem to notice.

"Drink," Sol said, and she drank until the container was empty.

In three abbreviated steps Sol was at the trash chute and discarded the container. He fished two more packets of red wine from a bin under the couch, not even bothering to check the variety, and, since he happened to be near the pill dispenser, he popped another blue pill. Two long bounds back to Jana and Sol lifted a corner of the blanket and slid in next to her. A wine container in each hand, he put his arm around her waist and gave her a hug.

"Don't listen to an old cynic like me," he found himself saying.

"No," Jana said, "the more I think about it, the more I see you're right. Jason's mother is an amazing manipulator, she never liked me, and...and..." Jana lapsed into silent tears.

Sol watched the cabin lights fade to starshine. He didn't credit himself with knowing a lot about women, about what went on inside their heads, but he had learned one lesson in his many years on two worlds: when a woman is crying, best to resist the male urge to try and fix it, to offer advice, to impose solutions; best to provide silent support, best to let her cry it out, as long as that might take, best for her to find her own solutions, her own way past the tears.

On the other hand, Sol's need for some kind of distraction was making him increasingly restless. In the dim starshine, the low ceiling seemed to hover just above his head. The walls – those stealthy bastards – crept a little closer every time he glanced toward the ceiling. He fidgeted, couldn't hold himself still. The wine and the extra pill seemed to be having no effect at all. His body was overheating under the flimsy blanket, even as Jana continued to shiver. His breathing was growing fast and shallow, despite his efforts to slow down and breathe deep.

Sol tried to distract himself by studying Jana's face. The starshine had erased her freckles, turned her skin to alabaster. He wiped away a tear before it could trickle into the shadow beneath her lovely high cheekbone; he tasted its delicate saltiness.

Jana was the distraction he needed.

He couldn't see her eyes well enough to know if she was looking back at him. He was pretty sure she was not.

Sol noticed that his breathing had settled down. Also, one of the wine containers was missing. And the one still in his hand was empty. How had that happened? Jana giggled as Sol's hands searched everywhere under the blanket. "What are you doing? What are you looking for?" "The other wine container." Jana held the container before his eyes. When he took it from her he found it was empty, too.

Jana was looking at him now, her eyes glittering. Foggily, Sol wondered how it could be possible for her eyes to glitter in the soft starshine. Jana wore a crooked, almost feral smile. And still her eyes glittered.

She leaned toward him and flowed over him like a long, low, insistent wave at high tide, so that Sol found himself on his back looking up into the shadow of Jana's body as she straddled him. He heard the zipper of her flight suit come down, watched as her arms writhed free, her body moving like a dancing Shiva. Then her hands were on his face, in his hair, and Jana was kissing him. She gave the slightest start — an almost inaudible intake of breath, an unseen arching of her back — when his own hands found her breasts. Her nipples were soft and slightly cool to the touch. With his fingertips, Sol traced gentle circles around the edges of her areolas. Jana's thighs were on either side of his waist, her bottom against his belly. She shifted now so that if they had both been naked Sol would have been in position to enter her. She unzipped his flight suit to the navel. Her hands slipped inside the fabric, her fingers playing with the hair on his chest, tickling the edges of his own areolas. She kissed him again, grinding her lips against his, but keeping her tongue primly behind her teeth, while at the same time thrusting and gyrating with her pelvis.

How drunk was she? Sol guessed she was pretty drunk. He guessed the same thing about himself. Plus that second pill was really starting to kick in.

"Take your clothes off," he heard himself say.

Jana stood uncertainly, pushed her flight suit past her hips and let it fall to the floor.

"I have to pee," she announced and drifted off toward the bathroom. Sol tried to remember if they had reactivated the bathroom fixtures after their excursion in the HyperWorld™. Evidently, they had not. After a few seconds of fumbling, Jana found the light switch and then a few seconds later Sol heard the bathroom fixtures slide back into place. "She can't be too wasted," Sol considered.

When she returned, Sol's flight suit was beside Jana's on the floor. Jana went straight to the wine locker. "More wine," she announced rather than asked or offered.

"Do you think that's a good idea?"

"I'm just afraid I broke the mood. I was hoping we could reset it."

Sol sighed. "Okay, let's reset the mood. Just one

container, though. We'll split it."

"Another blue pill?"

"Hell no."

Since the mood was broken and in need of resetting, Sol took the opportunity to also use the bathroom.

When they were settled once again under the gossamer blanket, passing the wine container back and forth in the fake starshine, it became apparent that Jana wanted to talk. About Kansas of all places. This was resetting a mood? But Sol was too buzzed to be anything more than mildly annoyed. *Let her talk*, a voice said inside his head; *Some women need that… What's the harm?*

They were half propped against the cushions of the couch, not in the wide, bed-shaped area where Sol had slept the previous "night" but in the space where Jana had slept, the part of the circular couch that had already become in both their minds Jana's space. Jana rested her head on Sol's chest. Her clasped arms, when it wasn't her turn to hold the wine container, circled his midsection. Sol's arm was around her shoulder, his hand moving lazily between her hair, the line of her chin, and the upper reaches of her breasts. Sol's other hand, when it wasn't his turn to hold the wine container, stroked her flank and her upper thigh, sometimes straying in slow gyres to the edges of her pubic hair. Their legs were intertwined.

It was becoming a contest between them to see who could take the smallest sip. Sol certainly didn't want any more wine; it was pretty clear Jana didn't want it, either. But Sol kept passing the container, kept hoping to bring the glitter back into her eyes. (It was remarkable how quickly she had sobered up.) And Jana kept passing the container back. What was she hoping for, Sol couldn't help but wonder.

She was describing her life growing up in some impossibly small town in Kansas – she had once before said the name of the place and just now said it again but Sol had already forgotten it – describing who she was before she met the boychik, Jason. Who Jana was had a lot to do with her family, apparently. But Sol was having a hard time concentrating on the details. She had a lot of aunts and uncles, a lot of cousins. A Mamaw This and a Granny That but only one papaw, as far as Sol could follow. She had a much older sister who was not altogether right in the head. Jana was not close to her sister, even though the sister – Sherry or Cheryl – had practically raised her, since their mother and father worked all the time. Her mother worked in a string of dollar stores and fast food restaurants; her father drove a truck.

Somewhere in the midst of all this family history, Sol had called a truce in the sipping game and set the wine container on the floor. This left both his hands free to explore Jana's body without constant interruption.

Unsurprisingly, the part he was most interested in exploring was between her legs. Jana let his hand stray where it would: she neither opened herself to him nor denied him. Sol was disappointed to find not the least hint of moisture, but as his fingers played with her clitoris and along the edges of her vagina they sent back signals to his increasingly foggy brain that perhaps there was reason to hope.

"Pass the wine," Jana said.

She did not sip this time but sucked the container empty. She embarked on a series of passionate kisses: kisses meant to seem passionate, anyway, as if she were trying to simulate passion with her body in order to convince her brain that this was something she really wanted to do: Sol felt this in his own body more than he apprehended it through the clouds that were forming in his head. She kissed his nose, his cheeks, his ears, his throat – anywhere but his mouth – and Sol found to his delight that Jana was much more playful with her tongue when she kissed him in these places. Her hand went between her legs and covered his hand, just as his middle finger was finding its way into her vagina. Jana moaned softly. The blanket fell to the floor. Jana's hand slipped beneath Sol's and she guided his fingers to all the places she wanted to be touched and showed him how to touch her and she sighed and her sigh became a long, deep, contented moan.

"I'd have never dreamed in a million years..." she whispered into his ear. And Sol knew what she meant: that her first time would be in such an unlikely place, with such an improbable man.

With her other hand, Jana stroked and fondled Sol's cock. It was not until she touched him there that Sol discovered his cock was curiously deflated. How was this possible? Jana seemed equally surprised and set to work righting the situation. But she really was quite inept when it came to giving a handjob. If anything, she was making matters worse.

Sol refused to panic. A man his age – he was talking real age here, not apparent – knew the key was not to panic.

"Turn on a light so I can see you," he said.

"A light?"

"Yeah, not too bright, just enough to see by, like candlelight or something."

Jana rose from the couch and adjusted the cabin lights to a faint pre-dawn glow. Sol watched her lithe form return to him, a nymph, a vision of beauty. But his cock remained unaffected. He started with her breasts because breasts often excited him: he fondled her, kissed and licked her, sucked at her teats. Nothing. He ravaged her in every way he could imagine with his hands and his mouth, exploring every inch of her. Nothing. Jana at first was highly aroused, then arousal gave way to bafflement, then bafflement to boredom and perhaps to wounded feelings.

At one point Sol arranged her so that she was lying on her back and he mounted her and attempted to enter her but it was no good, like trying to push a shrunken, floppy sausage into someone's ear. "Turn over," he growled and he attempted the same thing from behind with even less success, if that was possible.

The odd thing was – the scary thing was – as it went on and on, he felt the effects of the wine wearing off, so that he couldn't blame his monumental failure on the wine. Not entirely, at any rate. The blue pills were still having their effect, no doubt. How many had he taken? He couldn't clearly recall. But drugs like that had never caused this kind of problem for him before.

In the end exhaustion overtook him and he lay staring at the circular, slanted ceiling. His eyes stung, his mouth felt full of cotton.

"Turn off the lights," he said and she obeyed without a word.

When she returned to him on the couch, she covered them both with the flimsy blanket, cradled his head on her breast as if he were a little boy in need of comforting.

She spoke more of her small town in Kansas. Blue Mound was the name of the place. She did not speak now of her family or of other people from there. Instead, she described the look of the place, especially the landscape outside the town: the wide, gently sloping fields; the low scattered hills with their elegant curves; the vast, blue sky; the scarcity of trees; the way a lone tree could look so forlorn under that enormous sky; the sudden storms, as big as the horizon, as fast and as frightening as a plague of demons; the stars on a moonless winter night, the ghostly glow of the Milky Way.

Sol fell asleep with an image of rural Kansas in his mind. It felt like being in the HyperWorld™, except this was more vivid, more real.

Jana was nowhere to be found. Judging by the cabin lights, Sol guessed it must be about midday. It was now day four. He groped around in one locker after another, looking for a container of coffee. His hands shook, his head felt like a Martian sandstorm was raging just behind his eyes. His balance was none too steady. He found a container of coffee. French roast, black. Exactly what he was looking for. He heated it, sipped too fast, scalded his tongue. Swearing, he went to use the bathroom.

He found the door closed. He knocked but there was no answer. He figured Jana was in the shower and pressed the override on the lock. The door opened onto a large room with a parquet floor. Jana sat on a museum bench directly in front of him. Her back was to him and she was contemplating a painting from a distance, a Monet, depicting a bridge over a pond or a stream with flowers in it; Sol seemed to recall the flowers were water lilies. The painting hung on a wall perhaps seven or eight paces away.

"Do you mind if I take a leak?" he said. She gave no sign that she heard him. Sol searched with his hand along the surface of a wall he could not see. He activated the toilet which appeared to fold down out of thin air. The sound of him urinating echoed in the suddenly cavernous space. When he was finished, he glanced around. He recognized several impressionist masterpieces, all Monet's, then he recognized the room: they were in the Metropolitan Museum of Art.

Sol left the museum gallery, retrieved his coffee from the ship's cabin, returned. He eased himself onto the bench beside Jana. She glanced into his face and smiled weakly, resumed her study of the painting. She wore her flight suit; Sol was naked. He sipped hot but drinkable coffee from the plastic container. His dick stood at half-mast, rising quickly. "Stop that, you traitor," he scolded silently. His hands still shook, his head still pounded, his stomach wasn't so sure it liked the coffee. He was in no mood, absolutely no mood for sex, dammit. "Where were you last night when I needed you?"

"Hold this," Sol said out loud, handing Jana his coffee. He ducked out of the gallery once again, found his flight suit in a heap beside the circular couch, put it on, took a few deep breaths, and rejoined Jana.

She was still studying the same painting, the one of the footbridge arching serenely across a narrow, over-grown waterway. If it was a stream, the water must be flowing at a snail's pace for so many flowering plants to take purchase – but perhaps it was a pond. The bridge itself would not have been out of place in a Japanese tea garden. Sol seemed to recall that somewhere in France, perhaps on Monet's own property, there really was such a bridge, the work of some forgotten craftsman no doubt, and that Monet had painted it many times.

Jana continued to gaze at it, lost in thought.

"You like that one, huh?"

It took her several long moments to come back from wherever she had wandered.

"They're such compelling things," Jana said dreamily.

"What? The paintings? Yeah, they're nice," Sol offered. "Personally, I get a little bored after about half an hour in a museum. Give me the theater any day. Or a ballgame."

Jana smiled at him. "I meant bridges. But the paintings are compelling, too. I've been visiting museums all morning. I found files for dozens of them in the HyperWorld™'s database. I hope that was all right?"

"Sure, sure," Sol said, finishing his coffee. His hands were a little steadier now, although his head still ached. "That's what it's here for. Glad to be getting my money's worth out of the thing."

Jana frowned, blushed violently, turned away.

Sol was momentarily dumbfounded, then he got it. He started to speak, wanted to assure her he meant no reference to her, was not comparing her to the HyperWorld™ or calling her a thing. But his brain felt like mush, and the only words that came out of his mouth were a mumbled, "I didn't mean…I didn't mean…"

Jana relaxed slightly. She wasn't ready to forgive him, but she seemed to understand what he was trying to say. Sol thought now might be a good time to get more coffee.

He brought back one for Jana, too – café au lait.

"So, you like bridges?"

"I didn't say I liked them."

"You find them compelling."

Jana nodded.

Sol would have liked to stroll around the gallery, glance at the paintings, one after the other, then stroll rapidly through the next gallery and the next and the next until they were out of the Met altogether and on the streets of upper Manhattan. Maybe they could take a nice walk in Central Park: that would do his head a lot more good than all this fancy artwork. But Jana was still sitting on the bench. The HyperWorld™ was too cramped for him to stroll and her to sit, even within the confines of a single gallery: the perspective would get thrown off badly for one of them, perhaps both. Anyway, this program probably did not include the streets of Manhattan or the paths of Central Park or, indeed, anything outside the museum itself. Sol sat beside her.

Jana had not touched her café au lait, and it was only now that Sol remembered she had said she didn't drink coffee. What a dunce he was when he was hungover.

Jana mused, "Why do you suppose the artist cut off the ends of the bridge like that?"

Sol had no opinion on the subject, hadn't noticed that the ends of the bridge were not there to be seen in the painting. But now that he looked he saw what Jana was talking about: it was as if the bridge hung suspended in air above the water – the points where it touched the ground on either side were beyond the frame of the painting.

"I like it," Jana said, as if she had just reached an important conclusion. "It's a bridge you can just *be* on, does that make sense? You don't have to worry about what you're leaving behind or what's waiting on the other side."

"What would be the point of a bridge that didn't go anywhere?"

"I'm just being silly, I guess."

The first panic attack overcame Sol just as the cabin lights began their slow fade from late afternoon to evening. He had felt it lurking all that day, as if stalking him from the shadows in his own mind. He had attempted to elude it, first and foremost, by slow and deep breathing: "always a good thing to try when your head is going places you don't want it to go," according to Sol's grandfather. The breathing helped. Also — a trick Sol invented on his own — he looked at his hands. Sol had never told anyone about this trick of his because he knew it would sound to other people as if he were simple or demented. But in Sol's experience, when he found himself in a tight space, in an airplane for instance, if he looked at his hands, really looked at them, studied them, concentrated on them, he could sometimes put out of his mind the tight space he was in. It occurred to Sol that this was more or less akin to his grandfather's advice about heights: don't look down. In a tight space, don't look at the thing that is causing the anxiety, don't look at the space.

In similar situations and in the same way, Sol's notepad often proved a useful distraction. Except here, on this interminable journey, on this godforsaken craft someone had had the gall to christen the *Speedy*, Sol's notebook was practically no help at all. The trouble was: it wasn't connected to anything, it was cut off from communications with Earth and Mars and with anyone else who happened to be in between. As such, it was a dead thing to Sol. (Had he said this before, had he thought this before? He felt his mind, trapped in this space, was moving in smaller and smaller circles.) Worse, if he spent any time at all contemplating the notepad, it tended to drive home to him with surprising force how utterly isolated he was on this ship, how imprisoned.

Jana had ghosted around the cabin ever since tiring of her museum visits. She seemed to sense that Sol's mood was delicate. Or maybe she thought he was mad at her. She seemed to want to keep busy, making elaborate silent rituals out of the simplest domestic chores. Was she trying to demonstrate her usefulness to Sol, trying to give him his "money's worth" at least in terms of domestic service? Or was this her way of coping with her own fears, her own demons?

Sol wasn't exactly mad at her. He was growing wary of her, though, suspicious. He tried to go over in his mind the events of the previous day. How had he come to be so thoroughly hungover? By what steps precisely had he gone so far overboard with the wine and the blue pills? He had more than a vague suspicion that it was Jana's doing. How many times had she offered him one or the other? Or both? She had seemed so solicitous, so concerned for his well-being. But was there another motive? Was she trying to keep the old man incapacitated? Was this her way of trying to wriggle out of her bargain with him? Sol was startled to find he was seething at this thought. Keep the old man incapacitated: that was certainly her plot...and how well she had succeeded!...to Sol's utter embarrassment. What a conniver! How dare she?! But even as Sol seethed, another part of his mind was saying, *What...are you such a saint? Weren't you trying to get the girl drunk for your own purposes?* He wished he could remember clearly the events of yesterday. But his head was dull from the hangover, and the stomach-clenching dread that he could barely contain was making a jumble of his memory.

When the panic attack hit, Jana's first thought was that Sol was having a seizure of some kind or perhaps a heart attack. All the color drained from his face; he grew not just pale but ashen. He began to sweat profusely. He wrung his hands so forcefully, so incessantly that Jana, for an instant, was put in mind of an amateur actor overplaying the part of a Scrooge or a Shylock. Sol's eyes darted everywhere, all around the cabin, then toward his hands, then around the cabin again, then his hands again, and his eyes betrayed a hardness like diamonds, a glittering desperation.

"Sol?" Jana said tentatively; "Can I get you a glass of

water? Do you need some kind of pill?"

She could see that he struggled to control his breathing, skirting on the edges of hyperventilation. Between ragged breaths, he muttered then he ranted: he'd had enough, couldn't stand it another fucking minute, he needed to get out of there, he needed to escape.

Sol rushed to the entry hatch. For a sickening moment, Jana thought he knew how to open it. She had seen enough science fiction movies to know what would come next: they both would get sucked into the vacuum of space and die horrible deaths, their faces bloating, their eyes popping out of their skulls. Jana tried to drag him away from the hatch, but he fought her off with clumsy, distracted strength.

Jana looked around the cabin for something to hit him over the head with. By now she had figured out what was happening: it was his claustrophobia. Better to knock him unconscious than to get sucked into the vacuum of space. But the only thing she could see to hit him with was his notebook, which was nearly as thin and as light as a piece of paper. Useless.

She thought about the blanket. Maybe she could collar him with it, choke him a little if need be, and in that way drag him away from the hatch. But by the time she located the blanket, twirling it between her hands to give it a rope-like shape, Sol had abandoned his attempt to open the hatch and was trying to pry the front off the kitchen console, ranting now about finding hidden controls. He ripped off a fingernail in his frantic efforts, smearing blood.

Unfurling the blanket, Jana attempted to smother him in it and to tackle him. They struggled. To Jana it seemed almost as if they were engaged in a peculiar, awkward dance. Finally, she was able to tangle up her legs in his and trip him. He went down hard, knocking the wind out of himself, and she fell on top of him.

He barely struggled once he was on the floor. He seemed almost to take comfort from being wrapped in the blanket, from Jana's body on top of his, from her voice in his ear, desperately reassuring him that it was okay, everything was okay, calm down, calm down, we're almost home, everything's going to be okay.

Slowly, he got his breath back. The simple fact that he was no longer hyperventilating seemed a great victory.

Sol reclined on the wide part of the couch, the part he thought of as his bed, propped in a sitting position. It was the middle of the night by ship's time, but the lights were set to midday – Jana's doing, his request.

There had been three attacks so far. The first was the most sudden; the second was the most furious; the third one lasted the longest. According to Jana. Sol could not distinguish one attack from another: when they were happening he was, quite literally, out of his mind.

He had resisted using drugs and alcohol after the first two attacks – he was still feeling so puny from the excesses of the day before. But after the third attack, Jana gave him no choice. Before he was fully himself again, she force-fed him two blue pills like a seasoned veterinarian handling a sick, confused puppy. Sol sputtered and cursed at the time, and he still refused any alcohol, but he had to admit the pills were helping.

Jana perched on the couch a few feet away from him, her knees drawn up in front of her, eyeing him cautiously.

He had contrived to injure his hands. His knuckles were scraped, his palms and fingers were tattered. He had even somehow completely torn off a fingernail – from the ring finger of his right hand. It throbbed now, despite the antiseptic ointment and the bandage that Jana had applied. His ribs were tender. He was pretty sure he had twisted an ankle.

There were few signs of his rampages in the cabin itself. The place was all smooth surfaces, practically indestructible. Jana reported that he had attacked the entry hatch, multiple times, and the kitchen console – and the smears of blood in both places confirmed her report – but the objects themselves appeared to be undamaged. The only evidence of destruction Sol could see was in the corner of the couch that belonged to Jana. The cushions there were shredded, the stuffing pulled out of them, as if they had been set upon by a beast with dull talons.

Jana sported a scratch on one side of her nose, her hair was a mess, and there was blood on her flight suit. Sol had asked her several times already if she had been injured, and she assured him she was fine. She pointed out the blood on his own flight suit. She told him the blood on both suits was his. He felt disoriented, disjointed, unsure of his ability to read her, unsure if she was telling the truth. He hoped he could believe her.

He asked for the blanket and Jana told him it was on the floor in a corner. She made no move to get it. She did not want to relax her vigil over him for an instant.

"I'm doing a lot better," Sol assured her. "The pills were a good call."

Foggy though he was, on this score Sol knew what was in Jana's mind: if he showed signs of spiraling into yet another panic attack, she would pounce on him and try her hardest to get him in the restraints he wore during their initial high-acceleration period. It was a good idea, Sol had to admit. Even though it terrified him to think of being restrained: in his mind it represented one more layer of confinement, an extra dozen nails in the coffin he already felt buried in…but that was a bad image, that was an image he had to get out of his head right away: Sol breathed deeply, focused on his battered hands, cleared away images of buried coffins with the help of the billowing blue calm that the pills afforded him.

"I could really use that blanket," he said.

Jana studied him a long time. Evidently, she found him to be a safe risk. She unfolded herself and glided off the couch. Sol was relieved to see her moving so effortlessly, without sign of injury.

"Oh, it's got blood on it, too," she said.

She took the blanket into the bathroom; Sol heard the water start in the shower.

Jana returned to the cabin. "Give me your jumpsuit," she said.

Sol didn't trust himself to stand. Two blue pills and no booze were hardly enough to knock him off his feet, but he felt weak from the panic attacks – in particular his legs were shaky – and he did not want to appear frail in front of Jana. He stayed on the couch and squirmed out of his flight suit. He glanced at her face as he handed her the garment. He was surprised to find Jana frankly scrutinizing his physique, her eyes doing a slow pan from toe to top along the entire length of his body, lingering at about the halfway point. When their eyes met, she smiled. She might have blushed, but faintly. She disappeared into the bathroom.

Sol woke. He was under the blanket, lying down. Jana lay beside him. She held his head in her arms, her own head curling over the top of his. Sol had no idea how long he had been asleep, no memory of dozing off.

The lights in the cabin had been dimmed but not all the way to starshine. Was it dusk? Was it the hour before dawn? Sol tried to gauge if the lights were fading or growing brighter. After an indeterminate time, he concluded that they were doing neither.

Jana was asleep, he knew from the sound of her breathing, the slow rhythm of her heart. She was only partly covered by the blanket, and Sol could see that she was without her flight suit. In the pale light, her bra very nearly matched her skin tone but he could see that it was there, and in any event he could just touch the fabric of it with the tip of his nose; her lower half was covered. He did not have to glance under the blanket to know that he himself was naked.

The cabin was enormous. This was not a HyperWorld™ trick. The cabin was as spacious as a cathedral. And gravity was almost non-existent: many times weaker than, for instance, the gravity on the Moon.

Sol soared through the luxurious space, laughing. He spied Jana looking all about her, apparently confused, her size diminished by the distance between them. Sol landed easily in the wide expanse surrounded by the circular couch. "Watch this!" he called to Jana, and he sprung upwards with all his strength, gliding higher and higher until with his outstretched hand he was just able to touch the ceiling. "Bet you can't do that!" Sol felt like a kid.

With his next epic spring, he launched himself in Jana's direction. She watched him turn somersaults as his body described a long, slow arc. When he was near, Jana laughed and sprung into the air herself.

It became a game of catch. Sol was naked; Jana wore her panties and bra. Once she got careless, launching herself too high just as Sol had landed. This allowed him to gain ground on her with several short bounds and then to intercept her. He caught her on the way up while she was on the way down. They spun and grappled in midair. Jana struggled fiercely to free herself. Her bra came off. She scratched Sol on the nose and wriggled free.

"Gotcha back!" she called as she catapulted away from Sol, jamming her feet hard into his midsection, sending him spinning backwards head over heels.

The chase continued. Jana moved with effortless grace, like one of those gulls they had seen loitering nonchalantly in the tricky wind at the beach. Now that she was topless, her breasts rose higher on her chest in the low gravity, were rounder, less pear-shaped. Another effect of the low gravity: Jana's hair kept floating into her eyes and Sol could tell she wished she had something to tie it back with. Another effect: Sol's aroused penis wagged and wandered in every direction, like a compass needle gone mad.

Jana had learned quickly from her one moment of carelessness and Sol found he could no longer close the distance between them. He grew impatient. He wished the space were smaller, and the space grew smaller. Jana now darted one way and another, still eluding him. Now she was a dazzling fish in the ocean, sleek and sinuous. No mermaid ever swam with such allure. Sol wished the space smaller still, and the space grew smaller.

He caught her finally, pinned her to the couch. She struggled as before but her struggles only made her that much more enticing to Sol. She seemed to know this. He wanted desperately to get her panties off but feared that she would escape him. That's when the restraints built into the couch came into his mind, and one was there just at hand.

Until that moment it was possible to interpret Jana's struggles as part of the game. Now she fought in deadly earnest, flailing and bucking, writhing and kicking, but making not a sound. To control her, Sol rolled her onto her stomach. He sat on her, pinning her arms to her sides with his legs. His dick was an alarming sight, enormous, throbbing. He maneuvered one of her wrists into the restraint, activated it with the suddenly nearby keypad. Another restraint appeared. He did the same to her other wrist.

She continued to struggle and Sol stroked her naked back in an effort to calm her.

"Not like this, Sol" she pleaded, her face buried in the fabric of the couch. "Not like this."

He wanted to tell her that maybe it was better this way, that she could report truthfully to her boyfriend that she had resisted, that she had been forced. But the time for persuasion was passed. Now was the time for collecting on their contract, for taking from her what she had promised, however unintentionally, taking what he needed for his survival.

He grabbed a cushion from the couch and, lifting her, tucked it under her hips. She tried to kick at him; he shifted forward so that only her somewhat encumbered knees could reach him. She tried to twist off the cushion, a difficult maneuver the way she was tied, but just to be sure Sol held her firmly by her hips.

Jana grew still. Sol slipped his fingers beneath the thin elastic band of her panties and slid them slowly down. Jana swiveled her head as far as she was able and gave him a one-eyed glare. How wild she was, Sol thought, how impossibly young, how insanely beautiful.

The look in Jana's eye changed in a heartbeat from abhorrence to fear.

"Sol!" she gasped.

"I'll be gentle," he assured her.

"Sol! The cabin! It's closing in!"

He knew instantly that what she said was true. He had willed the space to grow smaller so that he could catch her. But once she was caught she was too much of a distraction, and he had forgotten to halt the shrinking of the cabin. Suddenly the walls came rushing toward him. He pushed against them with every ounce of strength he possessed. And so it was the ceiling, grinding downward as inevitably as death, that crushed him.

Sol screamed.

The cabin lights were still set to that dreamy uncertain time that was either dusk or the hour before dawn. Sol was desperate to know what hour it truly was, how many days, how many hours were left to endure. He reached for the keypad that would activate the screen in the ceiling above him, only to find that he could not move. The full set of restraints was on him: the wrist straps, the ankle straps, the wide strap that covered him from chest to belly, the straps across his thighs.

Jana's face appeared above him. "Oh dear oh dear, what am I going to do with you? It's too soon for another pill."

"I don't need a goddamn pill! Where's the keypad? I want out of this!"

Jana studied him.

"Sol?"

"What?"

"Are you awake?"

"Of course I'm awake."

"I thought you were before but you really weren't

and you did some very odd things."

"I'm awake now."

"I mean, you kind of went berserk. And just now you screamed."

"Just now I had a bad dream. I'm awake now."

Jana took a long, careful look at him. "I don't know what I should do," she said and drifted away.

So she had won. Perhaps this had been her plan from the start: hold him off as long as she could, then one way or another, while he was sleeping or panicking or under the influence, bind him to the bed for the duration of the flight. Now she could dose him as she pleased to keep him sedated. What a fool he was. He should have seen this coming. He should have deactivated the restraints or locked the keypads somehow. What a yutz.

He moved his head around now, searching for the keypad. It was well out of his reach. He tested the straps at his wrists; they were thoroughly secure. So were all the others as far as he could tell. He wondered what Jana would do if he said he had to use the toilet. Certainly, she had already thought about this, as it would have to happen sooner or later. Either she would rig up some kind of bedpan or else she would simply let him soil himself. Either way it was disgusting, and Sol did not want to think about it.

When Jana came back into view, Sol asked what time it was and she told him. It was day five, about an hour before Martian noon. Sol did some mental calculations. The total trip was eight Martian days — eight days, three and a half hours to be more precise. For the first twenty hours or so, Sol and Jana had been sedated and blacked out while the *Speedy* underwent its initial high-g acceleration period. There would be a corresponding de-acceleration period as they approached Earth, except the de-acceleration period would be even more severe and last about thirty hours. The de-acceleration period was set to begin at approximately two hours after Martian noon on day seven. Therefore, he could look forward to something like fifty- three Martian hours of incarceration before Jana would, hopefully, administer the drugs to help black him out for the final high-g phase of the journey.

The very idea of it caused him to break into a sweat, caused his palms to itch with anxiety. Two more days seemed like an eternity. Cooped up in this cabin was bad enough, but cooped up and *tied down* would drive him irretrievably insane.

Jana had drifted again out of his field of vision. She was wearing her flight suit. There didn't appear to be any bloodstains. Sol was still naked, covered with the blanket, which was also free of bloodstains.

Sol noticed for the first time that there was music playing: a soft, soothing jazz piece, elegant and uncompli-cated – piano, bass, drums. No doubt Jana intended this as a calming measure. Sol refused to be calmed.

Jana called from the bathroom, asking if there were programming instructions she could access for the HyperWorld™. Sol did not answer.

Jana's face appeared above him. "Sol? You okay?"

As calmly and as pleasantly as he could manage, Sol asked, "What do I have to promise to get out of this?"

Jana smiled. "I don't think it's a promise you could keep."

One biting remark after another passed through Sol's mind. He said none of them.

Jana said, "Tell me you won't have another panic at-tack. Promise."

Sol opened his mouth to speak, reconsidered, tried again. "I promise," he said.

"You big liar." Jana slapped him playfully on the chest.

Sol searched her face for any sign of prevarication. "Are you telling me I'm tied up because you're afraid I'll have a panic attack?"

Jana gazed at him, the image of wide-eyed innocence. "Why else?"

Sol continued to study her with deep suspicion.

"I'll promise you this," he said. "If I feel another attack coming on I'll lay down right here, I'll help you strap me in. I'll take any pill you give me."

Jana was undecided. "You really get crazy, you know?"

"I think the worst is behind me now. We're so close to home. Only two more days. It helps if I think about that."

Jana's brow furrowed. Could she tell he was lying? Did it matter? Sol kept up the sales pitch even though he knew it was almost certainly an exercise in futility. Jana would go on about his panic attacks, her concern for him, for his safety, how he was such a potential danger to himself. But that was just a smokescreen. Had to be. And they both knew it. They both knew what Jana's real motive was. It made Sol sick to play along with this farce, sick and weary. But there was that one chance that Jana was sincere in her concern for him. What were the odds? One in a hundred? One in a thousand? Ten thousand? A million? Well, it didn't matter what the odds were: it was the only chance Sol had. So he kept at it, tried every sales trick he knew, worked every angle, tugged at every hypothetical heartstring, and, incredibly, Jana slid the keypad into his hand. Sol activated the screen above the couch, read the release code, punched it in, and he was free.

They stood together on a red clay country highway. When they had first entered the program, Sol made the mistake of calling it a back road and Jana quickly corrected him: "in these parts this is a highway."

Great fuzzy tangles of white clouds crowded the blue sky: it was definitely Earth and not Mars. The land all around was flat and green.

"I thought you said there were hills."

"When did I say that?"

"The other day, when I was going to sleep, when you were telling me about Kansas."

"I didn't think you were listening."

The highway ran in a perfectly straight line for as far as the eye could see.

"There are hills. A few, anyway. But they're back toward Blue Mound."

They were in Coffey County, Kansas, a few hours' drive west of Blue Mound. Directly in front of them the road crossed a narrow ribbon of water by way of a simple, unraised concrete-and-steel structure with guardrails. Jana called this structure a bridge.

"When I was growing up," she said, "this was the scariest place on earth."

Programming the limited capacity HyperWorld™ to bring them to this little slice of nowhere had been a neat trick. Of course, the location did not exist in its meager database. Once Sol understood what Jana was trying to do, his advice had been to "find the closest thing and call it good enough...look, here's someplace in the generic images called 'Wheat Fields in Nebraska.'" But no, Jana wanted to show Sol a very particular stretch of highway in Kansas. "Okay, so go to the closest location in the database and see how far the range is." The closest real-world location had been the ruin of the Gateway Arch in St. Louis, with a range of no more than five miles for distant viewing of the memorial site: no help at all.

Sol mentioned how easy it would be if only they had access to one of those Whole Earth Imagining Sites on the web. Jana thought of Sol's notebook, and Sol reminded her that the notebook gave them no web access, that they were cut off, totally cut off from any and all outside communication.

"Calm down, Sol," Jana urged, pushing him gently in the direction of the couch.

"I'm good, I'm good," Sol assured her.

Jana would not give up on the HyperWorld™. "Hey, you know there is something in here that looks like Whole Earth Imagining. Whatever it is, it's in the program files, not the database. I don't see any way to access it."

Sol took a look. "Hmm," he said and got his note-book.

He told the notebook to connect to the HyperWorld™. There was some resistance from the HyperWorld™ but eventually the notebook won.

As it turned out, there were gigabytes of somewhat out-of-date Whole Earth Imagining data in the programming files of the HyperWorld™ that the HyperWorld™ didn't seem to be making any use of at all. "Sort of like DNA," Jana commented. "DNA?" "Sure, lots of info in DNA that maybe isn't so useful anymore but it never gets discarded."

Sol wondered briefly how Jana knew that but he was too engrossed in the programming problem to be side-tracked. He said, "The deluxe model has an anywhere-in-the-world feature that must use files like this. They must have turned it off for the limited capacity model. If we can only find a way to turn it back on…"

And so they did. And here they were in the proverbial middle of nowhere.

Sol could see right away why they had turned this feature off for the limited capacity model. The imagery was not quite right: a sort of blurriness at the edges of one's peripheral vision, a disconcerting "flatness" constantly interrupting the illusion of depth and space, a slight tendency of colors to bleed together, especially at the horizon where minute green mists spritzed into the uncertain blue fringe of the sky.

Also, the innumerable little touches of verisimilitude that one expected even from a limited capacity HyperWorld™ were missing here. Not a bee buzzed, not a bird sang, not a dog barked; the clouds in the sky were as still as if they had been painted onto a backdrop, and there was not the slightest breath of air, only an eerie, oppressive silence.

"Did something happen here?" Sol asked. That seemed to be the only explanation. "Did someone hurt you here?"

Jana shook her head.

"But this place scares you?"

"Not now. Not anymore. But when I was a kid, this place terrified me." Jana tried to put on a brave face but it crumbled immediately. "Okay, yes, even now I'm sort of scared of this place."

If there was a less intimidating spot on the planet, Sol could not imagine what it would look like.

"Maybe you were involved in an accident here, like a traffic accident, when you were very young and you have a repressed memory?"

Jana shook her head.

"Were you afraid there was a troll under the road where it crosses the creek? Like in 'The Three Billy Goats Gruff'?"

A nervous laugh escaped Jana. "I never liked that story. Maybe it made this scary old bridge scarier but that story wasn't the cause.

"Anyway, what are you talking about? That's not a creek, that's the Neosho River."

Trying to distract her, trying to put her at ease, Sol bantered, "You call that a river?...You call that a bridge?" Jana knew what he was up to, and Sol could tell that she appreciated the effort, and she tried as best she could to play along, but she remained nervous, uneasy.

A strand of hair fell across her face and Sol brushed it aside. "What scares you, then?"

Jana considered a long time, searching for words but also contemplating him, Sol – if she found the words, would he understand them?

"When I was really young," Jana mused, "I was scared of doors. Can you imagine? I don't remember being scared of doors but my Mamaw tells me I was, so I know it's true. Or maybe I should say doorways. Maybe it's more accurate to say doorways. I would not pass through a doorway of my own will. I had to be carried or dragged, kicking and screaming. I must have been a horrible child to live with. I must have driven my parents crazy."

Sol smiled uncertainly.

"Can't you see?" Jana said. "It's the same with bridges as it used to be with doorways."

"So, doorways used to scare you, now bridges do?"

"Not bridges, not in themselves."

"What then?"

"Crossing bridges."

She wasn't afraid they would collapse, which was Sol's first and only guess as to the reason why Jana would be scared of crossing bridges. She wasn't sure there was a reason. She was simply afraid of crossing bridges. Did Sol have a reason why he was afraid of tight spaces?

"That's different."

"How is it different?"

Sol had to grope for an answer. "Mine is more common, more natural."

Jana was unpersuaded.

If there had to be a reason, maybe it was that she was afraid of the other side. What was it like there? Would she get trapped there? Was she ready to leave behind, maybe forever, the familiar side she was already on?

"Okay, but why this one bridge in particular?"

In her corner of Kansas, anything remotely like a bridge was "few and far between." And when she was young, her family didn't move around a lot as a "family unit," in Jana's ironically annunciated phrase. "Mom and Dad didn't believe in it, I guess," she joked. Joking aside, the fact was: Mom and Dad were by necessity more into going to work and leaving the kids at home to fend for themselves. So Jana pretty much never traveled, never saw a bridge, except for on the internet or on television or worrying about them in nightmares. But her family did go as a unit twice a year to visit their cousins on Dad's side of the family, their Coffey County cousins: once in the spring and again for Thanksgiving. And there was this bridge.

"I wasn't always afraid of it. I couldn't have been. I must have crossed it several times as an infant and as a very small child. Maybe my fear of crossing bridges crept up on me as my fear of passing through doorways faded. I don't know, I can't remember.

"I used to really like my cousins in Coffey County – they're all scattered now: I don't see them anymore."

Sol said, "You scattered pretty far yourself."

Jana smiled but apparently could not bring herself to laugh in the presence of the fearsome bridge.

"They were all older than me and my sister, and you could tell they were a rowdy bunch, but they toned it down while we were visiting: they were very considerate, in their way. And Dad was always so happy there. Even Mom sometimes loosened up and enjoyed herself.

"Those visits, they should have been trips I looked forward to. And they were, or they would have been...except there was this bridge to cross.

"Mom and Dad never knew this bridge was the cause – I never told them – although they knew well enough that something about the trips to Coffey County terrified me. I wouldn't be able to eat for days before we traveled, both coming and going. I suffered from stomach cramps, headaches, nightmares. I often got carsick not far from this spot – and then, of course, my sister would get carsick, too. Boy, did that get Mom and Dad angry!"

The oppressive silence of the place was all around them.

Sol said, "We went to a lot of trouble to make this program. Since we're here, did you want to..." With a nod of his head, he motioned toward the bridge.

Jana gulped. "Sure," she said, trying to sound light-hearted.

They marched forward at a deliberate pace. Sol tucked Jana's arm under his. The loudest sound was the nearly inaudible *shoosh shoosh shoosh* of the fabric of their two flight suits rubbing against one another. As soon as they attempted even this slow advance, every problem with the holographic imagery became palpably worse. It made Sol's head swim. Jana, for her part, did not seem to notice.

The bridge could not have been more than twenty paces from end to end. They stopped at about the halfway point, leaned their forearms against the low rail. Sol was glad to see that the river was actually flowing: it made not a murmur, not a gurgle but it was the only part of the landscape that moved other than themselves. The Neosho was an unhurried river – its surface dull and unreflective, the slate gray water tinged with a coppery brown – but even so, on close inspection, it seemed to Sol that it moved in exaggerated slow motion: he suspected the HyperWorld™ had the water speed wrong.

"That river's a snake," Jana said, not without venom. "You should see how it writhes across a map."

Sol was still puzzling over this when Jana said, "I'm crazy, aren't I?"

Sol made vague reassuring noises to the effect that Jana was as sane as anyone.

Jana said, "I thought it would be easier to explain if I could show you this place. I thought maybe you'd catch a glimpse of it the way it used to look to me. But you know what's happening? I'm seeing it through your eyes instead. I'm seeing just how mundane and everyday this place really is. I'm seeing just what a…a nutjob I am: afraid of phantoms, afraid of nothing."

Sol turned to her. "What confuses me is: you knew what was on the other side of this bridge, and you knew you could always go back to the side you started from."

Jana gave him a sad, distressed smile, as if she felt sorry for him, as if he was missing something obvious.

"Every crossing changes a person, huh?" he said.

"Something like that," she said.

He didn't want to be the one to suggest they go on to the other side. He wanted Jana to be the one to say it. He was pretty sure she understood that. She seemed to be working it out in her head whether she would say it, whether she could. She looked like a mathematician grappling with a tangle of complicated equations, sorting through a viper's nest of interrelated values and relationships.

"That's odd," Jana said, and when Sol raised his eyebrows to enquire what was odd, Jana pointed toward the sky.

The once placid cloudscape was silently erupting into a massive confusion of roiling motion. Sol knew in an instant that no storm, not even a tornado, could shatter the sky like that. This was the work of...what? Celestial dragons? Colliding solar systems? Armageddon?

Sol was on the verge of attempting a joke, of asking if this sort of thing was usual for Kansas, when the whole vast landscape that surrounded them went suddenly black.

There was a tremendous crashing noise, and Sol and Jana were hurled violently against a wall of the *Speedy's* miniscule bathroom. Sol found himself pinned to the wall, as if held there by powerful, invisible hands. Jana sprawled across his chest, and the weight of her was grinding him into the wall, was crushing him. A flashing green emergency light above the bathroom door was their only illumination. Without warning, everything shifted and they were pinned side by side on the opposite wall, then the ceiling, then the wall again.

Jana scrambled toward the door but Sol held her

back. "Safer in here maybe," he said. Jana didn't agree. She thought the HyperWorld™ was malfunctioning and they needed to get out. "I think it's the ship," Sol said, "and I think it would be worse if we were getting tossed around the cabin like this." Jana still wanted out of the bathroom. She suggested they get to the couch, strap themselves in.

They slid from a wall to the floor and huddled there in a corner, waiting for the next disturbance – but none came.

Cautiously, they ventured into the cabin. It was dark there, too. Flashing emergency lights, green above the exit hatch, blue above the part of the couch where they could secure themselves. Silence, except for the hum of the ship.

Jana went immediately to the couch, put in place the wide strap across her midsection, and activated the screen in the ceiling above her. "The ship would tell us if something was wrong, wouldn't it?"

Sol wasn't so sure.

Jana resolutely worked her keypad, trying to communicate with the ship, trying to get any information she could.

"Can you turn those flashing lights off?" Sol wanted to know. "Can you make the regular lights come back on?"

"You should strap yourself in," was Jana's only response.

Sol knew she was right but he couldn't bring himself to do it. If the ship was seriously malfunctioning it probably didn't matter, anyway.

Sol rummaged in one of the food lockers and came out with two containers of his best wine, the brunello. He noted that there was wine enough for maybe four or five more days of normal consumption – (they carried extra rations of food and drink, despite the expense of the additional weight, "in the event of an emergency") – but this was the last of the brunello.

The emergency lights stopped flashing and the cabin lights came up to midday brightness.

"Good job," Sol said.

"It wasn't me," Jana told him.

Sol moved to join her on the couch. But before he completed his first step, an odd queasiness overtook him, then outright terror – the ceiling really was getting lower! – their space was shrinking!

The next thing he knew, Jana was beside him, speaking in a soothing voice, almost cooing in his ear, "It's okay, Sol, it's okay. The ceiling is right where it's always been…you're floating, that's all."

Had he spoken his fears aloud? He didn't think he had said anything but he must have.

"Let's get back to the couch," Jana urged. But before either of them could figure out how to do that, gravity returned and they landed in a heap on the part of the couch Sol had shredded.

"We've got to get ourselves strapped in," Jana said.

Sol had other priorities. "Where's the wine I was holding?"

Jana looked at him like he was crazy; Sol laughed and shrugged. Jana grasped him by the shoulders and, gazing earnestly into his eyes, said, "Sol, listen to me, I think you're having another panic attack. We've got to get you strapped in."

Sol laughed again. "Almost," he said. "Almost had a panic attack but I'm good now, I swear. Where's that wine?"

Jana, confused, retreated to the wide part of the couch. Sol located the wine containers; they were on the floor close to the kitchen console.

Jana had strapped herself in again and was working her keypad, staring at the display screen on the ceiling. Sol sat down beside her. "What's the news?" he asked lightheartedly.

Jana glanced at him. "I don't know how you can be so unconcerned."

"Is that screen telling you anything?"

"It says our status is normal, it says we're on course and on schedule."

"Well that's that then, nothing to worry about. Here, kiddo, have some wine."

An hour passed. Two hours. Jana finally relented and unstrapped herself from the couch. She sat up and Sol passed her one of the containers of brunello. They touched plastic containers together as if making a toast, and each took a sip. Sol had been waiting for her.

The cabin lights were still at full daylight. The ship hummed innocently along.

Jana wanted to speculate about the cause of the disturbance. Her own theory was that it had something to do with the HyperWorld™. They should never have messed around with the program files, should never have visited Kansas.

Sol was pretty certain that the HyperWorld™ and the operating system of the *Speedy* were completely separate, but he told Jana that maybe she was right.

Jana also wanted at least one theory from Sol, and he produced one. The *Speedy* was moving at fantastic speeds and therefore had to avoid collisions with even tiny particles of matter: a collision with a rock no bigger than the size of a marble would be catastrophic. Maybe the ship had detected something like that in its path and had taken evasive measures.

The more Jana went over the merits of that theory, the more she liked it. And Sol had to admit it was somewhat plausible. It explained the sudden changes in speed and direction. It even accounted for the ship's status screen reporting that everything was normal: an evasive maneuver like that possibly was normal for such a flight, was nothing to report. But for himself Sol was resigned to certain other conclusions.

It seemed likely to him that something was wrong with the ship: nothing like this had happened years before, on the way out to Mars. That first little disruption could well be the precursor to something worse and, at the speed they were traveling, even a minor malfunction was almost guaranteed to lead to sudden and catastrophic annihilation. It was probably something akin to a miracle that they had not already been destroyed. So, there was that: the threat of imminent extinction: each heartbeat could be their last – of course this was true for every person all the time, but who gave it any thought? – but how could you avoid thinking of it in a situation like this?

Worse still was a possibility he hardly cared to admit, but his mind kept coming back to it like a tongue probing a sore tooth. What if that little disturbance had knocked them off course? Perhaps instead of speeding toward Earth they were now hurtling in some random direction, further and further into empty space. If that was their situation, Sol had no doubt that they were moving too fast for any other ship to intercept them. They would die slowly, either from lack of food and water or from lack of air, or perhaps the cabin would lose pressure and they would be killed by their own bloating bodies, or perhaps the heating system would fail and they would freeze to death. Or perhaps they were now on course toward the sun and they were going to be cooked.

Sol thought the kindest thing he could do for Jana was to pretend for as long as possible that everything was going to be okay. The time when they would have to begin to face the reality of the situation would come when the scheduled de-acceleration period did not occur, assuming they were not already dead by then. Sol tried to figure out how many hours away that was. He found to his surprise that he couldn't make this simple calculation. He must be more scared than he realized. A day and a half, give or take, that was as close as he could estimate.

Evening was upon them but the lights of the cabin remained at midday. This upset Jana out of all proportion. For a minute Sol thought that maybe Jana would succumb to a panic attack of her own, and he couldn't understand why. He tried to calm her, offered her more wine, which she haughtily refused. He fiddled with the lighting controls until he got them to dim to something like sunset. Jana breathed a little easier. When Sol had a minute to think it through, of course her reaction made sense: she wanted so desperately for the ship to work like it was supposed to, for everything to be okay. Any little malfunction interfered with that wish. He would have liked to reassure her that everything *was* going to be okay, but he didn't think he could pull it off, didn't think he would sound sincere.

Sol tried to think of something mundane, something routine that he could do. He went to the bathroom for a quick wash up. When he returned, he found that Jana had prepared a meal for them.

She accepted another container of wine when they

sat down to eat, a very fine merlot. Sol attempted to make conversation. He asked Jana about her plans for when she got back to Earth, but this elicited long pauses and choked, monosyllabic answers. He tried to draw her out about Kansas, about her Coffey County cousins. This got a slightly better response. Jana even told a brief recollection of her Mamaw's who, as a girl, had seen the St. Louis Gateway Arch intact.

"Yeah, me too," Sol said.

Jana stared at him, surprised. "How could you have?" Jana wondered.

Sol quickly changed the subject.

Jana had very little appetite. Sol ate slowly, savoring each mouthful. The meal was another gourmet feast, the centerpiece of which was roasted Martian farm-raised trout in what Sol guessed was some kind of Velouté sauce.

"If we were back on Earth right now," Sol said, "and eating a meal like this in a fine restaurant, the waiter would be looking down his nose at us for drinking red wine. But I've never let some snooty waiter bother me, I'll drink red with anything."

Jana answered with a weak smile.

"But if you prefer white..." Sol said, realizing that he had not given her a choice at the start of the meal. "Would you care to switch to white? There must be a few containers of white around here somewhere."

Jana did not care to switch.

After she disposed of the plates, moving solemnly in the glow of sunset, Jana paused to select some music. Sol felt like a bit of a dolt for not having thought to play music while they ate. Jana opted for jazz again. But the playlist she chose now was not the same as the mellow stuff she had selected when she was trying to bring Sol out of his panic attacks. The music now had more heart and more edge to it, greater complexity, more instrumental voices, higher highs and lower lows. To Sol, still contemplating either a quick death or a slow one, it was the most exquisite music he had ever heard.

He suggested they go for a walk in the HyperWorld™. "Maybe the beach again or…" remembering how that had gone "or anywhere you like — but just some standard setting, no mucking around with the program files. And no bridges!"

But Jana was averse to the HyperWorld™ now. She wanted nothing to do with it.

She retrieved two more containers of red wine, sat on the circular couch at a spot about halfway between the wide part and the place that Sol had destroyed. She beckoned to Sol, enticing him with the wine. "Come here," she said, "and hold me."

The wine was forgotten once they were in each other's arms. They did nothing but sit together and hold one another while the ship hummed and the music took them places, each on their own solitary journeys. Time seemed to stop; the sun never quite got around to completely setting.

Jana said, "Tell me again that everything's going to be all right." And Sol told her it would be.

She snuggled against him as if trying to get even more entangled in his arms. "You don't believe it any more than I do," she said. Her face was pressed against his chest, and he could tell right through his flight suit that she was tearing up a little but also smiling.

She told him her fears about what would happen to them, and her fears were remarkably similar to his own. "For a while I wasn't sure you knew," she said, "so I tried to keep up a brave face but I don't think I was very convincing." Then, after a pause, she said, "I hope it happens all of a sudden, not the other way, don't you?"

Sol nodded.

"And I hope when it happens it happens quick."

Sol nodded again.

"But I hope it doesn't happen quite yet."

"Me either," Sol said.

If there was an instigator of that first kiss, Sol would have said it was Jana although, really, it was more as if the kiss happened of its own accord — and it did feel like a first kiss between them, despite all that had gone before. Sol couldn't say how long it lasted, except that it lasted a long time and not long enough. He felt a kind of tension in Jana's body that he had not experienced before: no longer that of a hunted creature but rather the tension of a coiled spring. He felt in himself not the usual predatory urge; instead, he felt…he had no easy words to express it…he felt the beginnings of a kind of peace that he could hardly name or describe. He'd heard once long ago of an unusual near-death experience: mountain climbers, for instance, who have fallen from great heights and survived often describe having a sensation while they were falling toward what they believed was certain death, a sensation of utter peace and acceptance, almost a mystical experience. Sol felt something like that now, the first hints of something like that. Partly it came from the very strong suspicion, the very near certainty that he would die at any moment. But more than that it came somehow from Jana, from being in her presence, from her warmth and her tension, from the scent of her.

Jana had endured a lot of trouble over the last few hours, a lot of stress, much of it thanks to Sol himself, and the scent Sol now perceived had nothing to do with any soap applied in a holographic shower, still less with any perfume, of which the *Speedy* carried none, but was the scent of Jana herself, her musk, her sweat, and Sol found it to be deeply alluring.

For a time, Sol kissed with his eyes closed and for a longer time he kissed with his eyes open. When he first looked, he found that Jana's eyes were closed. But it wasn't long before he found her gazing back at him – had she somehow been able to sense his gaze on her? The cabin lights, now stuck at twilight, turned Jana's pale blue eyes into opalescent pearls.

When that first kiss ended, Sol found he was hungry for air, as if he had forgotten to breathe. Jana smiled, slowly traced his lips with her finger, and when the tip of her finger came to rest in the center of Sol's lips, he kissed the tip of her finger.

He saw in her eyes both passion and regret. He would have liked to believe the passion was for him but he could see plain enough that was not the case. Jana's passion was for life, to live it, to experience it – not everything: nobody had time for that – but the main things, one of which was love, which maybe she had found the beginnings of with her boyfriend, her soulmate, her Jason, but time would not be given to her to ever know for certain; another of which was sex, which was still an available option, provided the ship held together long enough, even though the available partner was not of her choosing and not the man she would have chosen. Hence the regret. Or at least some portion of the regret.

What she saw in his eyes, Sol could only guess. He tried to hide nothing from her and he tried not to pretend. He was frightened, of course: he didn't want to die, wasn't ready for his life to end; he didn't want to die painfully; above all, he didn't want to have to watch Jana die – and at the moment all those prospects were very real. He wanted her. He knew that much must be easy for her to see. He had wanted her the whole flight, had wanted her from the moment he saw her photos in that catalog. He had wanted her at the start mainly to distract him from his claustrophobia. He wanted her now, still, partly to distract him from his fears. But he wanted her now for other, more powerful reasons, too. What those reasons were he couldn't exactly say. Partly it had something to do with the fact that she had withheld herself from him for so long. Whereas she wanted him so that she could experience sex, he wanted her simply to experience her. He was desperate to experience her before he died. Did he love her? He was pretty sure the answer to that was no, pretty sure that falling in love was a sport of the young, but he couldn't be certain — and now there was no time to sort out such a question.

Jana wanted another kiss. Sol was eager — not to say impatient — to get on to other things. But here was the one sure advantage that age had in a moment like this: Sol was not some callow ignoramus, charging forward, presuming that a stiff dick trumped all other concerns; Sol knew that Jana had to be the one to set the pace and, despite the perilous situation, Sol was able to find the forbearance to proceed as Jana wished.

Still, as this second kiss wore on Sol sensed in himself a growing restlessness. Jana seemed somehow less than fully present, and it both puzzled and irritated him. Was she growing bored? Was she *waiting*? Waiting for *him* to become the aggressor? That certainly wasn't the vibe he got from her just a moment ago. Then it suddenly clicked and Sol understood what she was doing: she was pretending he was Jason, imagining Jason there with her and not Sol, focusing on dreams and memories of the boychik, experimenting to see if his image would help her to give herself over more fully to what was about to happen. Sol was miffed – or, he knew he should be miffed, he wanted to be miffed, but he couldn't quite muster the sense of self-importance it would take to make the emotion real. *Let her have her own space inside her own head*, he told himself. *It doesn't matter*, he told himself; *she should pretend to be with whoever she likes.*

But before the kiss was over, Sol felt her come fully back to him. He sensed somehow that the experiment had been a failure and that her return to him was not altogether reluctant. Jana was with him, Sol, and with no one else. Sol was astonished at the way his heart leapt at the realization.

Jana's hand moved against his chest and slowly she urged the zipper of him flight suit down. Not all the way, not quite to his navel, but far enough so that her fingers could stroke the hair on his chest. Sol made no move yet to undress her.

Given the fact that each expected the ship to come apart at any moment, the pace of their lovemaking was perversely slow. There was no other way to describe it. But sometime during that last kiss a kind of wordless understanding had passed between them and each knew that the pace of their lovemaking was exactly right. Each trusted that the ship would hold together for as long as they needed – or no, it was even more irrational than that: each believed that magically they held the ship together, that it was not possible for the ship to come apart while their desire for one another remained unsatisfied. What might happen afterwards was beyond their ability to consider.

The music Jana had selected was a long and varied playlist and the jazz continued to flow, but it seemed to Sol that it was coming from very far away. Sol was only aware of it at odd moments, and in those moments it felt more like a warm, lazy ocean current than an auditory experience.

Jana's arms found their way inside Sol's clothes. An eon passed and Sol's flight suit slipped off his shoulders. Glaciers advanced and retreated, continents drifted, and Sol was naked to the waist. Another eon passed and Jana, too, wore her flight suit at her hips.

The time they spent semi-nude was a mere epoch. But what a lovely epoch it was from Sol's point of view, as he spent vast stretches of the period exploring Jana's breasts, discovering afresh those two enticing moles he had first seen in her catalog photo, then moving on to pay special attention to her nipples. He first scouted them with his fingertips, keeping his one bandaged finger tucked out of the way, then engaged in a thorough and meticulous survey with his mouth and tongue. Jana grasped his hair, spoke his name into his ear as he brought those delicious nipples to full arousal. But he couldn't keep her in that state. Each time she got there, something caused her to shy away, to withdraw inside herself. At one point, she pushed him backwards until he was lying on the couch looking up toward the ceiling. Jana straddled him and, bending over him, subjected his nipples to the same attentions he had given hers. It tickled Sol at first and he struggled against her, but Jana was determined, her mouth at once gentle and insistent, and Sol found that he came to almost enjoy what she was doing. It did not arouse him exactly but it sent small chills down his spine.

As she straddled him, Sol slipped his hands inside Jana's half-discarded flight suit and caressed her hips, her ass. She was not wearing panties, just as she had not been wearing her bra. Sol tried to think back. Had she been naked under her flight suit when they visited Kansas? How had he not noticed? But she must have been. It seemed an important thing to figure out, but Sol couldn't focus on it: Jana kept bringing him back to the present moment.

Sol was ready to move on to the next epoch, to dispense with the flight suits altogether, and he thought Jana was ready, too. He moved his hands to his own flight suit and eased the fabric lower until his fully erect penis sprang free like some pornographic jack-in-the-box. Jana recoiled. An abrupt awkwardness came between them. Out of the blue, they were like a pair of confused teenagers on a first date. It was absurd. Not to mention more than a little embarrassing, him sitting there with his dick wagging like a puppy's tail. Thank God the lights were low at least. Casting about for something to do, Sol found one of the forgotten wine containers and, punching in the straw, took a long sip and passed the container to Jana. As if desperately thirsty, her eyes darting in all directions except down, Jana gulped the remaining wine. Fine beads of sweat glistened on her chest and shoulders and among the delicate hairs on her arms.

"Do you remember the Golden Gate Bridge?" she asked.

"Of course," Sol said.

"I feel like I'm on it now — like *we're* on it — somewhere near the halfway point."

Sol sighed. "Still scared of crossing bridges, are we?"

Jana managed a guilty smile.

"I don't know how far I can go, Sol. Even now, I don't know how far I can go."

He took her in his arms and rocked her, told her she was beautiful, told her she was brave.

"You opportunistic bastard," she snorted into his chest.

"No! You are, you're very beautiful, you're very brave."

Jana allowed herself to be held but she kept her stomach pulled in and her back rigidly arched, avoiding all contact with a certain part of Sol's anatomy, and it did not take a genius to guess that she wished he would remove said certain part from her field of vision.

Sol left his dick right where it was. The Sol who boarded the *Speedy* what felt like a lifetime ago would have acted that way as a bargaining ploy, as a gamble in a tough negotiation: you don't bring the other party so near to the tipping point only to let them off the hook, you get them to the place where a decision must be made and then you keep them there until they decide. Those instincts were still present in his heart, to be sure. But now he discovered that his motives were different. Or, to be perfectly precise, he discovered that he had no motives, nothing ulterior, no hidden agenda. He simply did what he did. He didn't feel he had any choice in the matter. To do anything different, to tuck his dick inside his pants for instance, would have been dishonest somehow, would have been to pretend that he didn't ache for Jana in every cell of his highly perishable body.

If she flat out told him to put his dick away, that she couldn't go through with it, well that would be a different story, wouldn't it? But she had said no such thing. Or was her body language now — the tense stomach, the arched back — her way of saying it? Sol's penis began to sag; he felt very old, very mortal.

Jana reached down and gently circled Sol's penis with her fingers. She stroked him with infinite tenderness and he sprang immediately back to life.

"I think you like that," she whispered.

Sol let out a happy strangled sound that was meant to be a yes.

Jana took her hand away, brought her fingers to her

mouth and, looking Sol straight in the eye, licked them slowly and thoroughly, then resumed stroking him. The small chills he had felt earlier became delicious electric shocks.

Sol wanted desperately to touch Jana between her legs, to worship at her clit, to give her back some of the pleasure she was giving him. But he didn't dare make a move to take her clothes the rest of the way off. Not just yet, not in that moment. Instead, he kissed her, he ran his fingers through her hair. He licked the sweat off her shoulders, her breasts. He was sweating, too. He thought to himself worriedly, *It's getting hot in here*, but he said nothing.

All this time Jana had been more or less sitting on the tops of his legs. Now she slid off and crouching beside him removed his flight suit completely. His feet were pins and needles from lack of circulation but that only lasted a little while.

Jana flowed back onto the couch, creating a small distance between them, her fingers playing along the length of Sol's body. She studied him as intently as if he were a famous sculpture in one of the HyperWorld™'s museum files.

"You're quite a beautiful man," she said, her voice barely more than a whisper.

In normal life, Sol treated compliments the same as insults: he let them roll off his back without a second thought. And so he was entirely unprepared for the sudden rush of idiotic joy, or for the odd little lump in the back of his throat, caused by Jana's quiet comment.

She was propped on one elbow, taking in every detail of him. Sol watched her breathe, watched her ribs gently rise and fall. With one hand, he touched her cheek, he explored the delicate curves of her ear, of her neck, he traced the perfect line of her collar bone, he dallied in the sweet hollow between her breasts, while his other hand strayed to her hip and urged her flight suit lower. Jana ignored his attempts at this, not shifting her weight, not helping in the least. His hand found its way inside the fabric, his fingers insinuating themselves as far as the edge of her pubic hair. She was touching his cock again, this time lightly tracing the sides of it from tip to base, her hand lingering at the base so that her pinky and ring finger could play with his balls. He strained to reach between her legs with his own hand and Jana relented a little and the flight suit inched lower; he made the faintest contact with her pubic mound.

When Jana abruptly shifted her body so that her hips slid down to about even with Sol's thighs and his hand lost ground so that it hardly reached past her belly button, his heart sank: she'd lost her nerve. His hand only stayed inside her flight suit because the flight suit itself rode up nearly to her waist. Sol felt almost sick with disappointment. But when Jana shifted a little further and her head came even with Sol's crotch, a wild hope flared in his mind.

Her fingers still played idly up and down the shaft of his penis. She seemed mesmerized by the motion of her own hand. Her eyes looked as white as moonstones in the pale light. Sol, too, was mesmerized. Music entered briefly into his consciousness, a cool tenor sax riff, and it seemed for a crazy instant as if Jana somehow was producing the sound through the motion of her hand. She turned her gaze toward him and gave him a long, questioning look. Then she bent her head, her lips parted ever so slightly, and she took his penis into her mouth. Just the tip at first. It was almost more of a kiss at first. Then her lips spread further apart and made themselves into an elegant lascivious oval and with exquisite slowness she swallowed more and more of him.

She was unpracticed, that soon became evident – Sol was willing to believe she had truly never done this before – yet the pleasure he felt brought him as near to ecstasy as he had been in decades, maybe ever. He couldn't explain it. She had no sense of rhythm or timing; she made no use of her tongue; she seemed at first to think it was important to get every inch of him into her mouth and so she kept gagging herself: she learned quickly to stop doing that. In short, she was a complete amateur, and somehow that made it wonderful.

When Jana's hair fell in front of her face, Sol gently tucked it behind her ear. He desired very earnestly to watch. Jana's hair wouldn't stay put so Sol continued to play with it, to brush it out of the way. He resisted the urge to take hold of her head and to guide her movements. But the urge didn't last long. Partly because Jana was taking cues from his body and she soon didn't need that sort of guidance: she was noticing the things he liked and doing more of those things. She learned, for instance, to give special attention to the tip of Sol's penis, which caused him again and again to shudder with delight.

Sol lay along the edge of the long curving couch; Jana was between him and the backrest. In his excitement he found he was crowding her against the backrest. He tried to stop but the problem only got worse. Jana glanced up at him wide-eyed. With a sick feeling in his stomach, Sol realized that the problem was not his doing at all but another shift in the gravity of the ship. Jana must have already understood this. She was gagging again, his penis being forced deeper into her mouth. She twisted away, sputtering. He grabbed her shoulders and pulled her toward him until they were face to face. For an instant, they lay on the backrest as if it were the seat of the couch. Or, rather, Jana lay on it and Sol was on top of Jana. He rolled off of her, afraid he would squash her, and was almost flung over the top of the backrest: only the fact that they were clutching each other so fiercely prevented him. In the next instant, they toppled back onto the seat of the couch, the ship's gravity having returned to normal.

They huddled in each other's arms, breathing rapidly. Sol could feel Jana's heart thumping. He supposed his was doing the same.

"Another change in direction," he said. He tried to sound nonchalant about it but he knew he wasn't fooling anyone.

Jana looked about to cry and, not knowing what else to do, Sol kissed her: he put everything he had into it. Jana held back at first, letting Sol kiss her only because she thought he needed solace. But as the kiss went on, she found she needed solace too – and they both put everything they had into that kiss.

Jana's clothes came off. They wrestled each other to the wide part of the couch and frolicked there in the more open space. Sol thought from time to time that he felt them floating: whether this was the ship's gravity going haywire again or simple euphoria Sol had no way to tell.

As before, Jana orgasmed so gracefully, so effortlessly: Sol brought her off with his mouth, then with his hand, his fingers working side by side with Jana's. She made several attempts along the same lines to get him to go off but Sol withstood every onslaught.

The hum of the ship had grown to a dull, grinding roar. When had that happened? Had it been all of a sudden or a little at a time? The music was no longer playing. Or perhaps the sound of the ship was drowning it out.

Sol felt a creeping conviction that this was it, that in a

matter of minutes he and Jana would be reduced to smithereens and space dust. He chided himself that he should become more urgent in his lovemaking but, strangely, even now their lovemaking moved at its own pace: he kissed Jana, he tasted her and drank her in, he petted her and groped her, he strummed her like a living instrument; and she did the same to him. They went at it with an exigent intensity Sol had never experienced before and yet there was a quality to it of – not careless-ness exactly, not languor, or not merely those things – more a quality of playfulness, of contentment.

And yet – Sol could see it in Jana's eyes – she felt the same as he did, that time was of the essence.

The look on Jana's face was heartbreaking. She was so young, she had so much still to experience, so many bridges still to cross – terrifying though they might be for her. And now she had to endure the terror of losing the time to cross those bridges, the true terror of dying. Sol wished he could give her more time, would gladly have volunteered for extinction if only one of them had to die and one could be saved. Instead, all he had to offer her was a last-chance means of crossing one of those scary bridges, a small slice of the life she wouldn't get to live.

She smiled at him. Her eyes sparkled in the meager light. She touched his penis, guided it between her legs. She squeezed his sides with her knees, invitingly, encour-agingly. He placed his hand on top of hers, nuzzled the edges of her vagina with the tip of his penis, then, taking his hand away and taking her hand with his, raising her hand to his mouth and kissing it, he pushed gently forward and felt the warmth of her, the moist yielding flesh. He placed his hands on the couch on either side of her to position himself to fully enter her – slowly, delicately.

The pressure of her knees against his ribs became abruptly strident, like she was trying to hold him in place. Sol cooed to her to relax. "Sol?" Jana said in a small, alarmed voice. His hands and knees lost contact with the couch. Sol and Jana were floating. Worse, they were floating apart.

For one mind-bending instant it was as if Sol had been here before – déjà vu! Then he remembered his recent dream.

He and Jana scrambled to reestablish their embrace. But weightlessness was tricky: it seemed as if the slightest wrong move pushed them further away from one another. Jana grabbed Sol's hand; otherwise, they would have lost all contact.

The cabin began to spin.

"What's happening?" Jana cried.

Sol guessed that the spinning objects were actually he and Jana, that some kind of centrifugal force was acting on them. His feet scraped a wall of the cabin. He folded his legs up as tight as he could; Jana did the same.

"Just hold on!" he called. He was afraid that if their hands parted they'd each be flung to an opposite wall.

The force pulling them apart grew stronger, the cabin spun faster. Meanwhile, Sol's greater weight was pulling them "off-center," and it was only a matter of time before they collided with something – a wall, the ceiling.

Sol got a crazy idea. He knew it was crazy, he knew it had zero chance of working, and even if it worked it probably wouldn't make any great difference, but he did it anyway. "Strap yourself in!" he roared and with that he flung Jana toward the couch. He aimed her a little ahead of the wide part, figuring that her momentum would carry her to the target.

Sol's head crashed into the ceiling and he lost consciousness.

108

**

Jana's face was above him. Momentarily, he couldn't bring her into focus. But he knew the face was hers. She was smiling, beaming at him. "Hey you," she said; "you're back."

His head felt like someone had used it for the anvil in a game of Martian screechhammer.

"Why aren't you strapped in?" he wanted to know.

"No need," she said and pecked him on the cheek.

He was lying flat on his back on the couch and he wasn't strapped in either. He tried to sit up but that made him feel sick to his stomach and he gave up the attempt. Solicitously, Jana placed a cushion under his head.

Jana wore her flight suit. Sol appeared to be naked. The gossamer blanket covered his midsection; he could see his feet and hairy lower legs sticking out the other end. The cabin lights were set, he guessed, to midmorning.

"The ship's behaving itself?" he enquired doubtfully.

"The ship's fine! We're going to be fine!"

Sol nodded without conviction.

"No really, Sol, it's true. But if you don't believe me there's someone from the transit company waiting to talk to you. He can explain. Are you up for it?"

Sol's heart sank. There was no way for anyone outside the *Speedy* to be in communication with them. Jana must have cracked under the strain. He set about attempting to explain the situation to her as kindly as he could.

Once Jana understood what he was trying to say, she cut him off with an exasperated smirk. "Here," she said, "you can explain to the president of the transit company how *he's* crazy, too."

She disappeared from above him. A moment later he

heard her voice: "Mr. Calhoun, are you still there? Oh good. Yes Sol...um, Mr. Vincente can take your call now." The screen above Sol's head came to life.

Sol saw a balding, middle-aged man wearing an expensive silk tie and an executive suite. He introduced himself as the president and CEO of the Mars Transit Corporation before launching into a long string of nervous apologies.

Sol interrupted, "How are we even talking, Mr. Calhoun?"

Mr. Calhoun blinked at him, not comprehending the question.

Sol said, "How are you able to get a message through? I thought that was impossible."

"Ah," said Mr. Calhoun, catching on. "Of course you're right, Mr. Vincente, sir, it is quite impossible... or it was, when you were traveling at what we call slip-speed. But now that you've been de-accelerated..."

"De-accelerated? When did that happen?" Sol demanded.

"Oh dear," Mr. Calhoun said; "Have you been unconscious the whole time, sir? I see the bandage on your head, sir. Are you very badly injured? Your, er, assistant didn't tell us that you were injured."

Sol touched the side of his head and, sure enough, there was a bandage there. It seemed to go all the way around his noggin. More apologies flowed from Mr. Calhoun, whose eyes kept wandering to the top of Sol's head.

Sol had dealt with a hundred guys like this – at least a hundred, maybe a thousand. A corporate big-shot through and through, he probably treated everybody beneath him like dirt, he had that air, but he became an abject toady when in the presence of someone like Sol, a member of

110

the owner-class.

Now he was going on about the period of de-acceleration. "We compressed the thirty-hour process to sixteen hours, sir, it must have been quite rough, I'm terribly sorry, but there was no other way, we had to de-accelerate you as rapidly as possible. So, maybe it was a good thing you missed it?"

Sol glanced at Jana. She wouldn't have missed it. "Was it bad?" he asked her. Jana just smiled and shrugged.

In response to the question "What went wrong?" Mr. Calhoun was a hard man to pin down. The "incident" was still "under investigation." They had not completely ruled out the possibility of "pilot error."

"What pilot?" Sol asked. "Are you telling me there's a pilot on this crate?"

"Ground control," Mr. Calhoun amended. "An error on the part of ground control. Possibly."

In midflight, well past the halfway point, the ship had "somehow" gone off course: the only way to correct the problem had been to drop them out of slip-speed and set a new course. Sol sensed that this corporate lackey knew very well the cause. Was it gross incompetence? Could it have been sabotage? Sol wondered how well the ground control team had been vetted. Oh, just wait till he was in touch with his Earthside lawyers: the lawsuits they would bring!

Meanwhile, Mr. Calhoun was going on at great lengths about the technical difficulties of prematurely dropping them out of slip-speed: something about a new method of breaching the communications barrier, highly experimental, never attempted before, how it had failed on their first two attempts, how it was absolutely a marvel that it worked at all.

"So when do we get out of here?" Sol wanted to

know.

"Er, as to that," Mr. Calhoun stammered, "as to that, let me assure you, Mr. Vincente, sir, that we've done a complete inventory of your stores and you should be fine..."

"My *stores?*"

"Yes, your supplies...you know, food and water and such. A complete inventory, as I say. Your – ahem – your assistant has been very helpful."

Sol wanted to reach through the screen and grab this bastard by the throat: he couldn't stand the snideness that crept a little more into the toady's voice each time he referred to Jana. Sol supposed he had been away on Mars too long: he had forgotten what prigs Earthmen were compared to Martians.

"Mr. Calhoun," Sol said. "Has my companion been fully informed of the situation?"

"Er, yes sir, I believe so, sir."

"Good. Then I'll let her fill me in. Stand by, I'll call if I have further questions." And with that Sol broke the connection.

He turned to Jana, studied her. She looked tired, haggard. "How bad was it?" he said; "tell me."

"It doesn't matter, Sol. We made it through, that's what matters."

"Were either of us strapped in?"

"We were both strapped in."

"How did that happen?"

Jana had not landed on the wide part of the couch where the straps were, as Sol had intended, but at least she landed more or less on the couch, so she had a soft landing compared to his. Before she even hit the cushions, she watched Sol collide with the ceiling. "You're head snapped forward so hard I was afraid you'd broken your neck," she reported. The collision caused Sol to ricochet off the ceiling. He turned one somersault in the air and, miraculously, landed square in the middle of the wide part of the couch, faced entirely the wrong way but at least on his back. While she was dragging him into position to strap him in, Jana noticed that his head was bleeding. It wasn't gushing but she thought she'd better bandage him. Meanwhile, the ship's gravity was gyrating wildly and growing increasingly intense. Anything not secured was zipping every which way across the cabin. A container of red wine exploded against a wall. "I had to get us both strapped in in a hurry," Jana explained. "I used the nearest thing I could find for a bandage, it just happened to be floating past."

Jana stared at him with mirthful eyes. She giggled.

"What's so funny?" Sol asked.

"Oh Sol," Jana said, laughter spilling out of her. "I forgot all about it."

"What?" Sol demanded.

Jana was clutching her sides, trying to contain the laughter. "I really should have changed that bandage before I let you speak to Mr. Calhoun," she gasped.

Sol examined the bandage with his fingers. He pulled it free. It consisted of Jana's panties stretched over the top of his head like a shower cap, held in place with a few ragged strips of material hurriedly torn from a flight suit.

They had de-accelerated from slip-speed and the ship did not have the fuel or the capacity to re-enter that state, not that Sol or Jana would have wanted it to. The rest of the transit to Earth would have to be accomplished at standard speeds. The good news was that the *Speedy* for the most part had done its job and they were tantalizingly close to Earth: no more than about two and a half times the distance of the Moon. The bad news was that, at standard speeds, this still left them about eight days till they reached near-Earth orbit and could rendezvous with a shuttle.

Sol fought hard against the feeling that they were right back where they started. Objectively, he knew that this was not the case. But that did nothing to quell the old panic welling up inside him.

At least their "stores," as Mr. Calhoun called them, would hold out, although it would be a close call: almost certainly they would be reduced to white wine before the end of the trip.

Also on the plus side, there was no longer a communications blackout; therefore Sol spent hours on his notebook, following events and tracking his holdings on two worlds. In an odd way, though: he watched from a distance without meddling, without messaging. Not his style at all.

The automatic dimming and brightening of the cabin lights no longer worked. Jana tracked the time through the screen above her position on the couch and adjusted the lights manually.

The HyperWorld™ was also toast. Sol had tinkered with it to no effect for an hour or so that morning, after a shave and a shower – thank God basic holographic bathroom functions were still operational. Jana expressed relief to be rid of the HyperWorld™, but for his own part Sol felt uneasy about losing such a potentially useful distraction.

For the time being, ground control was doing a good job of keeping their acceleration constant, thereby creating something akin to normal gravity inside the cabin. But ground control had warned them that there would be a period of weak gravity and then weightlessness lasting several days once the ship reached maximum speed. Sol silently fretted over the possibility that the additional disorientation would further inflame his claustrophobia.

He wasn't expecting much help from Jana on that front. Jana had grown pensive, distant. Talk about being back at square one! Sol tried to convince himself that he was merely disappointed by this development, nothing more. Certainly no one should say that he was devastated: it would be a gross overstatement to say that he was devastated.

Sol peered and peered at his notebook's diminutive screen – and the factoids and news items, the endless array of numbers, graphs, charts, statistics made less and less sense.

His need for her, he told himself, was entirely situational: without the looming panic he would have no need for her at all. None.

Sol kept replaying in his head how Jana had seemed the first few moments after he had regained consciousness: the "hey you," the peck on the cheek. Then there occurred the unpleasant conversation with Mr. Calhoun – more accurately, the conversation with the unpleasant Mr. Calhoun – him with his "ahem"'s and his smarmy innuendo. But Sol didn't think that was the cause of Jana's new frostiness. She seemed fine right after, more than fine: oh, how they laughed about the panties! They fell all over each other laughing. They laughed because they were still alive; they laughed to wash away the proximity of death, the fear of it. They laughed till they cried.

What was it, then? What was the cause?

Well obviously, she no longer believed that she was in immediate danger of being turned into space dust. Her future had been restored to her and she wasn't about to muck up the present with an old lecher like Sol Vincente. Perhaps it had taken her a little time to process the new situation, perhaps the "hey you," the peck on the cheek were nothing more than left-over momentum from those desperate moments before the de-acceleration.

Sol sighed. He glanced all around the cabin, irrationally hoping to catch site of Jana, knowing full well she was in the bathroom. She had been in there a long time.

The change seemed to come over her soon after the last spasms of laughter died away. They were holding onto each other, Jana in her flight suit, Sol naked: the blanket had fallen to the floor. He was gazing at her; she was looking everywhere but at him. "This place is a mess!" she exclaimed and sprang to her feet. She set about putting the cabin in order. Sol made motions to help. "You should get dressed," she said. He found his flight suit in a heap by the exit hatch. The left arm was missing, torn off at the seam – by Jana, no doubt, when she was bandaging his head. He did as he was told and got dressed. "This feels weird," he said; "maybe I should tear off the other arm, too." Jana acted like she didn't hear him.

It was her right, Sol supposed, sighing again, to act any way she pleased. He didn't have the heart to go back and re-read their contract but he was pretty sure that the agreement, specific enough about services to be rendered, clinically specific in some of its articles, was sketchy at best as to duration. Jana could well argue that her side of the contract was only binding for the initial eight days of the voyage. Beyond that, it could be argued, Jana's responsibilities were at an end and she had at least partially fulfilled her side of the agreement; it still remained for Sol to fulfill his: they were not yet back on Earth.

Sol would have wagered half his Martian holdings that Jana wasn't thinking along those lines. But there it was. Any lawyer worth his salt would tell her as much.

It was this stray thought about lawyers which caused Sol to realize that, as far as he knew, Jana had not been in touch with anyone beyond the ship, not a lawyer, not a member of her family, not even the dubious Jason. Of course, it was possible that she had called someone while he shaved and showered...

Was that it? Had she gone behind his back? Had she been in touch with a lawyer? With Jason? The screens were there in the ceiling for her to use whenever she liked.

"Gone behind his back"? Where was *that* coming from? Sol feared he would not last another eight days: he had no doubt he was going stir crazy.

Jana emerged from the bathroom. Sol put on a false smile, eyed her suspiciously. Her flight suit looked freshly washed; so did her hair. The skin of her face was pink and well-scrubbed. Obviously, she had made use of the shower. Did that explain all the time she'd spent in there? Sol didn't think so: you could take three showers, three long showers, in as much time as she took. *Who knows?* Sol thought, *maybe she's figured out a way to turn the HyperWorld^{TM} circuits into a communication device.* He frowned at his notebook screen.

They had finished dinner before Jana disappeared into the bathroom, and by the ship's clock it was now well into the evening. The cabin lights were still midday bright, however.

Jana glanced all around the tiny cabin. "Did you do the dishes?" There was no mistaking the note of astonishment in her voice.

Sol shrugged. "Trying to keep busy."

Jana dimmed the lights. "Is that too dark?"

"It's fine," Sol said; "the screen makes its own light."

Jana perched on an edge of the couch. The ship no longer hummed as it did when they were at slip-speed; instead, from beneath the floor came small rumbling sounds like the drums of a distant marching band, also quick intermittent swishing sounds not unlike the hiss of a furtive cat. Ground control had assured them that this was normal.

Jana said, "Too bad about your notebook."

"Huh?" Sol said. "What?"

Above the sounds of the ship, Sol heard music. Jana must have just put it on.

"Oh nothing," Jana said. "I was only thinking that if you could have communicated through that notebook the whole time, you wouldn't have needed any company at all."

Sol set the notebook aside. He peered intently at Jana. Her face seemed partly lit by pale fire, partly hidden in shadow.

"What did you set the lights to?"

"Full moon."

They studied one another as the ship labored on and the music played.

"I know that tune," Sol said. "The Drifters, 'Up on the Roof.' Do you know it?"

"I think I might have heard it before."

"It's what they call Classic Americana these days. My granddad loved that kind of music, he used to play it for me when I was a kid – he listened to it when *he* was a kid and it was retro even then. I love this stuff, too."

"Guess that explains why there's a whole playlist of it on the ship's computer."

"Guess so."

After a pause, Jana said, "I can't see you very well in this light. Why don't you come closer?"

They didn't embrace right away. They sat side by side, touching each other's faces, lightly running hands along each other's arms and legs.

"That flight suit does look sort of silly with one arm missing," Jana observed.

Sol would have liked to make some quip but the words wouldn't arrange themselves in his head.

"You had me worried, Jana," was all he could manage to say.

"I had some thinking to do," Jana said, understanding him perfectly.

He thought he should tell her that the contract between them was no longer in force: he wanted to be sure she knew that. But he hardly got a word out before she stopped him from speaking with first a finger to his lips and then a kiss.

"Eight days," she murmured. "What am I going to do with you for eight days?"

Sol recognized the next song, too: Sam Cooke, "Everybody Loves to Cha Cha Cha."

V.J. Quinn lives alone in a book-lined house beside a creek in the Southern Appalachian mountains.